Raising the Last Dragon

Raising the Last Dragon
By Joe Broadmeadow

Copyright

ISBN Print: 979-8-9927210-8-9

ISBN ePub: 979-8-9927210-9-6

Table of Contents

Destiny Set in Motion

"The choice is made."

Ealdor's voice once again surrounded them. Duncan looked at the egg.

"What happens now? Is it over?"

Balinor came forward, bending down to put his face next to Duncan. "It is only beginning, Donnchadh Ealdgneat."

Duncan tilted his head, eyes narrowing on his friend. He knew whatever Balinor was trying to tell him would mean more challenges. As if what he had faced hadn't been enough.

Kathy and Jamie came over while Keladry revived Myrddin, then joined them, standing around Duncan and the egg.

"Jamie, what happened to you?" Myrddin asked. "Last I remember, you tried to fly."

Jamie chuckled. "I grabbed Harper, and then something happened. We fell over the edge but didn't fall all the way. Something held us in the air. She tried to push me away. One of my hands slipped, and I felt myself starting to fall. I realized whatever was holding us up was just interested in holding her. I was just along for the ride and decided to get away from her. I saw the branch and leaped for it."

"What happened to Harper?"

"I'm not sure. A bunch of ravens flew in, and she vanished among them. I wasn't sure what was happening up here, so I waited. After a few minutes, I felt the branch starting to give way. I started yelling for help."

Myrddin glanced at Keladry. "She's still out there, isn't she?"

Myrddin nodded. "What matters is the egg is safe in the hands of the Dragon Seeker."

"What do we do with him?' Kathy said, pointing at Core.

Keladry spoke up. "That spell won't hold him for long. He is too powerful for that. We must get away from here."

"And just leave him?" Kathy walked to face Core. "Isn't there something a little more unpleasant we can do?" She eyed the sword, watching the unmistakable sign of fear in his eyes. She reached for the blade.

"No!" Duncan said, drawing their attention. "We're not like him. There is nothing he can do to us now. We need to focus on this," pointing at the egg. "This is the *LAST* Dragon. We need to protect it, not become like those who would misuse its power."

Ealdor's voice once again rose from the pulsating egg. "Donnchadh Ealdgneat shows wisdom beyond his years. Heed his message."

Myrddin nodded his head. "We would do well to listen to her. This is the future we have all fought for long and hard. Much remains for the Dragon Seeker to do; there are many trials ahead. Core and his allies failed; that is punishment enough…for now." With a wave of his hand, Core disappeared.

"Where'd he go?" asked Duncan.

Myrddin smiled. "Someplace where he will no longer trouble us, at least for the immediate future."

Duncan once again took his place on Balinor's back; the egg secured in his pack. As the others moved off down the hill, the sun crossed over the mid-point in the sky.

A gleaming beam of sunlight illuminated the river, the water a shimmering, twisting band of gold. Pointing to the future.

Balinor leapt into the air, riding the light. Duncan felt the rush of the wind in his face. The smell of the woods enveloped him. The sun warmed his back.

"An uncertain future awaits you, Donnchadh Ealdgneat." Ealdor's voice sang in his ears. "You've taken the first steps of a long, difficult journey. For now, protect this egg and this dragon within. The next challenge will soon be upon you."

Duncan took comfort in the voice yet trembled at the portent of the words. These once uncomplicated and familiar places of his life, the Blackstone River, the rocky face of Diamond Hill, and this small town of Cumberland, would never be the same.

His imagination opened to the possibilities. He knew what he needed to. He would face his fear and overcome it. It would not be easy, but it would be a destiny of his own choosing.

The End of the Beginning…

Chapter 1   Making Adjustments

Duncan opened one eye as he felt Tripod burrowing down into the blankets.

"Hey," Duncan pushed back, "get back down the bottom where you belong."

Tripod looked at Duncan, put his paw over his head, and turned away, ignoring the command.

Sliding to a more upright position, Duncan could see the problem. Taking up the bottom of the bed was a sleeping dragon. Twice the size of Tripod, the dragon slept soundly away, lying on her back, arms and feet in the air, while little puffs of smoke rose with each exhaled breath, oblivious to the rest of the world.

He smiled, patting Tripod on the head. "Sorry, buddy, you've been displaced."

Tripod whimpered, then buried his head deeper in the covers.

Duncan slid over to offer more room, resting his head on the pillow and his hand on Tripod.

I'm gonna need a bigger bed…

*****

"Duncan," his mother yelled, "get down here or you'll be late for school."

Duncan struggled to pull himself out from under the blanket. It wasn't easy with a dragon sprawled out, pressing his full weight on everything. Even a juvenile dragon weighs a lot, and this one ate everything in sight.

Duncan tugged at the bar as Tripod nudged the sleeping dragon, a low growl rising from his throat.

"It's alright, buddy, I got this," Duncan said, as his legs slid out from under the covers. Keeping the momentum going, he swung his legs into his chair and slid his body into the seat. Rolling to the closet, he pulled out some clothes.

"Duncan, let's get a move on." His mother's voice, a blend of humor and impatience, echoed up the stairs.

"Coming, Ma, just getting dressed."

Duncan knew his mother was standing at the bottom of the stairs, fighting the urge to bound up the stairs and help him. But he knew she understood his need for independence and privacy. Even if the real reason was that he needed to keep the dragon a secret.

Something that was becoming harder and harder to do.

Dressed and ready, Duncan nudged the dragon.
Nothing.

Tripod growled, trying to look like a lion ready to pounce. Balancing on his one front paw, weaving back and forth on the bed, he did not make an imposing sight.

The dragon burped. A small puff of smoke escaped from her lips as she curled away from Duncan's prodding and poking.

"Let's go, let's go," Duncan said, using both hands to bounce the dragon in the bed. "You can't stay here, move it."

Raising its head, one eye still shut, the dragon nodded. Shaking herself awake, she stepped from the bed, walked to stand next to Duncan, then faded into invisibility. Unless one stood right next to her, the air shimmering like an out-of-focus image, she was invisible.

Except to people who knew of her existence.

But for everybody else, who'd be looking for an almost invisible dragon next to a high school sophomore in a wheelchair with a three-legged dog?

Chapter 2   An Unexpected Expectation

"Hey, Duncan, over here," Kathy Craigendoran yelled as she spotted Duncan rolling toward the school entrance. Some of the senior boys noticed the head cheerleader and class genius calling out to the king nerd. What was it about that guy and Kathy?

No one understood how these two became close. Perhaps if the dragon appeared hovering over Duncan, or if Kathy conjured up some of her magic, they might understand and be more cautious in their uncomprehending stares.

Following along behind Duncan, dodging around the students oblivious to her presence, the dragon perked up at the sound of Kathy's voice. Speeding Duncan along with a quick flap of her wings, blowing papers out of the hands of Ms. Wächterin, the new English Lit teacher, the dragon landed silently next to Kathy, nuzzling against her.

"Hey," Duncan said, "that wasn't very smart," glancing at the now increased number of students watching him.

Kathy chuckled, stroking the dragon's head. "She is just happy to see me. Nobody noticed."

"Nobody noticed?" Duncan shook his head. "Half the school just watched me cover a hundred yards in about two seconds. I'm pretty sure they noticed. Not to mention that the new teacher chasing her papers all over the front of the school."

"Nonsense," Kathy said, as a smile crossed her face. With a simple flip of her hands, all the students staring at them suddenly lost interest, turning back to their own jitters for the first day of school.

Just as Duncan relaxed, a short gust of wind blew several sheets of paper onto his lap. Their arrival coincided with the new teacher grabbing them from him. She towered over Duncan, which was no surprise since he was sitting, but she was a good head taller than Kathy, and Kathy was a tall girl.

Her eyes seemed two different, if difficult to describe, colors, her nose pointed, and her hair a wild mix of undisciplined chaos. She was someone you'd never forget once you'd seen her up close. Not scary, just, well, unusual.

Duncan grew concerned the dark forces might already be back after them again. Was she one of them?

"What crazy weather you have here in Cumberland," she said. "I'm Ms. Wächterin, the new English Lit teacher. And who are you, young man?"

"I'm, ah, Duncan, Duncan Emeris...I, ah, I think I may have you for one of my classes."

"And you, young lady, who might you be?"

"Kathy Craigendoren, Ms. Wächterin. I'm in your class as well."

"I see," she said, but her attention seemed to be behind the two friends, not on them. "Perhaps we were meant to be introduced by the wings, I mean, winds of chance." She smiled, winked at Duncan, nodded to Kathy, and sauntered off to the entrance.

Kathy and Duncan watched her leave, then looked at each other.

"You don't think she saw her, do you?" Duncan asked, tilting his head toward the dragon.

"No, I don't think so," Kathy answered, looking to see where the dragon had gotten herself to. "You worry too much. They wouldn't send another one disguised as a teacher. We'd be onto them right away. Where is she, anyway?"

"Right behind me," Duncan swiveled in his chair. But the dragon was nowhere to be seen.

"Oh no!" Kathy said, "Look."

Duncan turned back toward the entrance. Ms. Wächterin was just walking in the door, the dragon right behind her sniffing at her hair as she batted away at the invisible nuisance.

"Hurry, Duncan, we've got to stop her before something happens."

They weren't the only ones troubled by the dragon's freelance entry into the school. Merrill Templar, also known by his Dragon realm name, Myrrdin, a former English teacher and one of Duncan's main allies in protecting the dragon, watched it all unfold.

He stood at the entrance, arms folded over his lanky frame, wire rim glasses poised on the end of his nose as if ready to leap off, bushy eyebrows forming an almost perfect pair of question mark bookends, tapping his right foot as Kathy and Duncan burst through the door.

"Slow down, Mr. Emeris. One inexplicable display of speed per day is enough. The dragon is fine, just curious. Your job is to train her, Duncan, not imprison her. Teach her the skills she needs to meet your next challenge, but let her explore the world.

"I think Ms. Wächterin is harmless, but we still need to protect the dragon from all uncertainty."

Duncan and Kathy breathed a sigh of relief. If Mr. Templar wasn't worried, no need for them to be either.

"And Duncan," Templar said, "have you come up with the name yet?"

Duncan shook his head. "Why do I have to name her? Isn't her name Ealdor? Like when I found the egg."

Mr. Templar's eyes glanced quickly around the area, then he leaned down to Duncan. "Reread the message from Keladry. Everything you need is in it."

"I have, Mr. T, a hundred times, but I don't understand what Keladry wants me to do. How am I supposed to figure out what to call her?"

Templar smiled. "Reread it, then again if you have to, and again, but the Dragon Seeker's first duty after finding the dragon egg and guarding it until the dragon emerges is to name her." He put his hand on Duncan's shoulder. "This you must do so we can prepare you and her for the next challenge."

Templar turned to Kathy, whispering something in her ear.

She shook her head. "I haven't quite figured out how to tell him," she said, glancing at Duncan.

"Tell me what?" Duncan asked.

Templar smiled. "These things are often best handled by just saying it." He tilted his head at Duncan.

"TELL ME WHAT?" Duncan said, getting anxious with all this secrecy. "I am right here, you know."

Kathy looked Templar, then at Duncan, then back at Templar, who nodded again.

"You have to name her now," Kathy blurted out, "so we can start picking out the names for the other dragons."

"Other dragons? What other dragons? You told me she is the last dragon."

Kathy knealt down next to him and put her hand on his. "Duncan, she is not the last dragon, she is the *L A S T* dragon. The *LAST* dragon comes from an egg hidden to protect the dragons from being exterminated. Whenever dragons face war or disaster, an egg is chosen and hidden away, awaiting the arrival of a Dragon Seeker.

"She remains hidden, holding all the memories of those dragons who came before her, until a Dragon Seeker helps her restore the dragons. They bear the responsibility of naming her, protecting her, teaching her, and helping her bring dragons back into the world.

"It's a way the dragons preserve themselves in the event of war or disaster."

Duncan tried to take it all in. The whole story of his being a Dragon Seeker was hard enough for him to accept, it had almost killed him and his friends. Now he was responsible for a whole race of dragons.

"But wait," he said, "I may not be a biology whiz, but I understand enough about it to know one dragon cannot reproduce. Where are these other dragons gonna come from?"

Templar chuckled and started back toward his new office as principal. "You've got it from here, Kathy. Break it to him gently."

Kathy watched Templar disappear into his office, then turned to Duncan.

"You're gonna be a daddy, the *LAST* dragon is born pregnant. You have to name her and all her dragon children. Bye." She ran off down the corridor, leaving Duncan to his thoughts.

"A daddy? I can't even drive a car. How am I gonna take care of a family of dragons?"

Chapter 3   What's in a Name...Everything

Duncan rolled into his house and rode his father's invention up the stairs to his room. His mom and dad were out, so he had time to himself. The dragon amused herself by sneaking up on Tripod, while invisible, and pulling his tail, sending the dog into spasms of barking trying to locate the mischiveous tormenter.

"Will you stop that?" Duncan said, causing the dragon to reappear. She sidled up to him, put her head on his lap, and sighed. Tripod moved to put his head on Duncan's lap too.

"You two need to get along," he said, rubbing both heads. "We are in this together."

Tripod let out a snort. The dragon sighed.

"What is my name, Donnchadh Ealdgneat, what is my name?" she said, using Duncan's other name known only to those of the dragon world.

"I'm working on it, but it would help if everything wasn't a riddle." Reaching into the hidden compartment in the arm of his wheelchair, he pulled out an old piece of parchment.

Torn on edges, brown with age, the words he'd read over and over stared back at him.

I, Dragon Seeker, am now deep in your debt
And there be one more task for you to be met
My true name is needed, you must not forget
Do not tarry long in choosing my name
Everything has purpose if reason remains
Say what is needed
Think what is nigh
In spite of the challenge
No burden am I
You will see what to do, on this we rely

The words mocked him. He understood a name meant everything, even more. But how was he supposed to figure out what name to pick when it would determine the future?

He scratched the dragon's head, and she fell promptly asleep. Tripod nudged him to keep petting him too.

"How is it I've come to this destiny?" he said, though no one was listening.

As the words came out, the dragon opened her eyes. "What did you call me?" she asked.

"I didn't call you anything. I was just…" and the light went on. "Destiny, your name is Destiny because we share the same fate."

The dragon smiled. "Destiny, of course, I knew you would get it right."

"How?" Duncan asked.

"Because the name was right in front of you, as is our entwined fate. See the truth, Duncan. Don't look for it, *see it.*"

And there it was, plain as day. He had only to open his eyes and *see.*

I, DRAGON SEEKER, AM NOW DEEP IN YOUR DEBT

AND THERE IS ONE MORE TASK FOR YOU TO BE MET

MY TRUE NAME IS NEEDED, YOU MUST NOT FORGET

DO NOT TARRY LONG IN CHOOSING MY NAME

EVERYTHING HAS PURPOSE, WHEN REASON REMAINS

SAY WHAT IS NEEDED

THINK WHAT IS NIGH

IN SPITE OF THE CHALLENGE

NO BURDEN AM I

YOU WILL SEE WHAT TO DO, ON THIS WE RELY

Chapter 4   Controlling Destiny

"Destiny," Templar said, his hand on Duncan's shoulder. "Of course it is Destiny, my boy. I was beginning to think you wouldn't figure it out."

"Why does this have to be so hard?" Duncan asked.

Templar eyes narrowed on the boy, eyebrows curling once again into a question mark.

"I know, I know, because if it was easy even Jamie could do it."

At the sound of his name Jamieson Haworth perked up. He had been engrossed in a text message, ignoring the conversation to that point. Duncan's best friend, he had once proven his great courage at the risk of his own life saving Duncan and the egg. In Duncan's class, Jamie was as loyal, if absent-minded, a friend as they come.

"Hey, what's that supposed to mean?"

"It means, Mr. Haworth, that we all have skills and limitations. Yours are extraordinary. Particularly your limitations." Templar said.

"Thanks, Mr. T, I think," resuming his focus on the messaging app.

Duncan smiled. "Okay, Mr. T, now that I figured out the name, what's next?"

Templar grinned.

"Oh, of course, I have to figure that out as well, right?"

"Not exactly, Duncan. Not exactly." Templar pointed toward Destiny flapping her wings and blowing a soccer ball away from a gym class working outside.

"Train her?" Duncan asked.

"Train her," Templar nodded. "Take Jamieson with you. He can be bait."

Jamie's head never lifted off his cell screen. "I heard that. I'm not playing bait for an untrained dragon."

Templar, with a slight nod toward Duncan, smiled. "You've got some time before your next class. Try something simple, like fetch."

Jamie looked up just in time to see the dragon land at his feet, sniffing him up and down.

"He's got the scent, Duncan, ready?" Templar said.

Duncan nodded.

With a quick glance to make sure no one was watching; Templar made a subtle gesture with his wrist. Jamie vanished into thin air.

The dragon pranced and danced around; the game was afoot, and she wanted to play.

"Ready, Destiny?" Duncan asked.

Bouncing up and down on her hind legs, the dragon stared intently at Duncan's hand.

"Okay, okay," he waved his hand, and she was off. "Bring him back, but remember," he shouted after the flying dragon, "he's my friend, not lunch."

The dragon, and Duncan's words, faded into the clouds. Duncan looked at Templar. "I hope she finds him quickly."

"I hope she remembers not to eat him," Templar said. "Having such conversations with parents, trying to explain how their child became an unintentional snack for an invisible over-eager dragon, are always a challenge."

Then he broke into a laugh.

"I imagine they are, Mr. T, I imagine they are." Duncan settled in to await Jamie's return, hoping his friend would be in one piece, not traveling separately through a dragon's digestive system.

What kind of destiny would that be?

Chapter 5   Dragon Training

As Duncan searched the sky for Destiny, he felt a presence. As if someone were watching him.

I'm never gonna get used to this magic stuff, how can I know things wh… A shadow across the sun interrupted his thoughts. Shading his eyes from the glare, Duncan looked for the shadow's cause.

Seeing nothing, he resumed his wait for Destiny. A subtle breeze brushed the back of his neck. Turning around he faced something unlike anything he had ever seen, and he had recently been inundated with the weirdest things in his life.

A creature, with the head and wings of an eagle on the body of a lion, walked slowly towards him.

Duncan grabbed the wheels of his chair, pushing himself back.

"No need to fear, young Emeris," the creature said, her voice soothing and bright. "I come to place myself at your service." The creature now bent her front legs and bowed.

"Wha, what, what are you?" Duncan asked.

"Some know me as a Hippogriff. We have a long history with the Dragons, sometimes contentious, sometimes beneficial, but we have awaited their return with hope."

"A hippogriff? I've never met a hippogriff."

"Well," said the creature, "until just a moment ago, I've never met a Dragon Seeker with wheels."

'I don't have wheels; this is my wheelchair. I can't walk."

"I see," said the creature, "no matter. You are the Dragon Seeker are you not?"

"I am," Duncan said, thinking how he wished this were not the case.

"Well then I am at your service." The Hippogriff bowed once more. "I will always be nearby; all you need to do is think of me and I will be by your side."

She, for Duncan had the distinct impression it was female, glanced around nervously as if looking for something, or someone, watching them.

"There is one thing you must remember, though."

"What's that?" Duncan said, glancing around himself, the creature's tension contagious.

"Many of us have long awaited your arrival and longed for the return of the dragon," looking from side to side once more. "But some of those creatures who may pretend to be your friend are not. They have been corrupted by those who would prevent the restoration of the dragon.

"While I will be here to help you, I can do no more than offer my advice. You must decide the course of your actions."

Why is it always my problem, Duncan thought, always an impossible decision between a bad choice and a terrible one.

"Because it is your destiny."

Duncan heard the creature's voice in his head, but she didn't appear to be talking.

"You can hear my thoughts?"

The Hippogriff nodded.

"And I can hear you in my mind?"

Another nod.

"So, you'll know I need you without me having to say anything, just think?

A smile crossed the creature's face. "That's all you have to do." The unspoken words soothing in Duncan's mind.

"I appreciate your help, whatever you can do," Duncan said. "Can you at least give me a hint about what to look for?"

"I will tell you this," the Hippogriff said, raising her wings as she prepared to fly. "You've heard the expression *beware of Greeks bearing gifts?*"

"Yeah, I know the story. We read about the Trojan Horse in history."

"Well, beware of any gift that seems too good to be true." The Hippogriff nodded once more and leapt into the air. "Be careful in whom you put your trust," her words fading as she flew away.

Duncan watched her disappear into the clouds then thought about what she said. Great, now I gotta be paranoid about everything. How am my supposed to call for help when I don't even know her name....

His thoughts were interrupted by shouts from a familiar voice. Spinning around in his chair he saw

Destiny hovering at tree height above the ground, Jamie dangling by his jacket from the dragon's mouth.

"Tell her to put me down," Jamie yelled. "NOW!"

Duncan shrugged. "Okay, Destiny, put him down."

The dragon hesitated for a moment, then released Jamie into the air. As he fell, his scream echoed off the walls of nearby buildings. Just before he hit the grass, Destiny snatched him once again, placing him on the ground.

"Oops," Duncan said, a smile crossing his face.

"I could've been killed," Jamie said, brushing himself off and glaring at Duncan and the Dragon. He lunged toward Duncan but was lifted off his feet by Destiny.

"Yeah, but you weren't. Calm down or I'll play another round of retrieve the dummy with Destiny."

Destiny, hopping and spinning Jamieson round and round, seemed to relish the idea.

"Okay, okay, enough already, I'm getting dizzy," Jamie said as Destiny released him. "I suppose I should be happy she didn't eat me for a snack."

"That's it," Duncan laughed, "keep a positive attitude. Now we better get going to class. Don't want to be late on our first day."

Chapter 6   Reasonable Suspicions

Rolling into the classroom, Duncan followed Jamie as they headed toward the desks in the back.

"And where do you two think you two are going?" a voice challenged them as they made their way through the maze of desks.

Turning to the sound, they saw a tall, gaunt woman, arms folded, head tilted slightly, tapping her foot. Her hair, curly and golden yellow, surrounded her head like a mane. Her voice sounded like a young woman, but deep brown eyes, creases running from each side, and a face seasoned by the sun gave her an appearance that said older.

"Misters Emeris and Jamieson I presume.," she beckoned with her finger for them to come forward. "I've been forewarned of you two by some of your former teachers. I've reserved these two desks right in front of mine…" She paused for a long moment, letting her words settle in. "Where I can keep an eye on you."

Jamie exchanged glances with Duncan, then they both looked back at the teacher.

"You must have mixed us up with someone else." Jamie offered with a big, if insincere, smile.

"Hmm, of course. Let me wait for two other students who look just like you and with one of them in a wheelchair. An understandable confusion." Her face took on a more serious look and she gestured with her eyes for them to sit at the desks.

Jamie almost collapsed in his chair as Duncan rocked his wheelchair back and forth to get at his spot.

"That's what I like. Instant, unquestioning obedience." She turned and walked to the chalkboard. "Let's keep it that way and we'll get along famously."

"Yeah, you might but we won't," Jamie whispered out of the corner of his mouth.

"Oh yes you will, Mr. Jamieson," the teacher said, without turning around. "Or we'll be spending lots of extra time together in detention."

"You heard that?" Jamie said, then thought better of it.

"I hear everything, young man, and I can read your mind, so be careful what you think."

Jamie looked at Duncan. Duncan shrugged.

"But from what I've been told you'll ignore my advice and try anyway," she said. "Some people just learn the hard way." She grabbed a piece of chalk and wrote, *Ms. Seherin*, on the board.

Turning back to face the class as the rest settled in. "As you can read on the board, my name is Ms. Seherin. I know you were expecting someone else for this history class, but things changed.

"We will start by studying Ancient history from the beginnings of the first humans. One of the most important things we will study, and practice, is the art of storytelling. From the moment the first humans gathered around the fire, telling stories was how they passed down history and knowledge.

"I understand many of you like to write," she glanced at Duncan and held his eye for a moment. "In this class we will mix the skills of reading about the past with creating our own imaginative stories about it. You will tell these stories in class. They will be told from your imagination, not read word for word.

"I want you to experience the sights and sounds of those times long ago, under skies filled with stars, surrounded by the sounds of the wild, as the old and the young, men and women, friends and strangers told stories before the firelight.

"When the weather and time permits, we will have several classes held outside under those same stars, before our own fire, and recreate the same moments experienced all those thousands of years ago."

"We have to come to school at night?" Jamie said, almost without thinking.

"Well, and here I thought you were a bit dull, Mr. Jamieson. Yet you figured out for us to see the stars we would require darkness," Ms. Seherin said. "There is hope for you yet."

Jamie groaned, then caught himself.

"Consider it bonus to your education. And you need all the bonuses you can get if your reputation matches reality. Now where was I?"

Silence descended on the classroom as the dread of public speaking permeated their brains. While it was true Duncan loved to write—writing got this whole dragon thing going on the first place—telling stories to others wasn't high on his list of things to do. He liked the idea but still had butterflies from the thought of eyes watching him tell a story.

He had no problem reading his own words to others, but this wasn't the same. This was something different.

As Duncan began to settle into the class while Ms. Seherin spoke about the first humans in Africa, his heart jumped to high speed as Destiny came sailing into the classroom. While she was invisible to most, she still could wreak havoc.

And just as those thoughts entered his mind, she did just that. As Destiny floated past Ms. Seherin, she misjudged the space between the teacher and her flying trajectory. One wing tapped the back of the teacher's head as she wrote on the board.

Ms. Seherin spun around and saw Jamie, who could see the dragon, chuckling. Glancing down at her feet she spotted the tip of a pencil eraser. Reaching down to retrieve it, momentarily hidden behind the desk, her voice emerged before she did.

"Mr. Jamieson," she said, rising to her feet and holding out the eraser tip, "is this your idea of a funny prank?"

Jamie 's eyes grew wide. "I didn't do that. I'm not crazy."

Seherin twisted the eraser round and round in her fingers, eyes narrowing on Jamie. "I will give you the benefit of the doubt...this time. But tread lightly, Mr. Jamieson, tread lightly."

Jamie let out a sigh of relief and pretended to throw himself into intense writing of notes. Duncan glanced over and had to control a smile.

On his paper, Jamie had written, *Seherin is cuckoo. Seherin is cuckoo*, over and over as he tried to calm himself.

Meanwhile, Destiny had settled onto the edge of Ms. Seherin desk, making faces at her and moving papers around when she wasn't looking. Duncan tried to catch Destiny's eye to make her stop but she ignored him.

As the bell rang, the class made their way toward the door. Jamie was the first one out. As Duncan made his way, he glanced back to make sure Destiny was following him. The dragon sat immobile on the desk staring at the teacher and Seherin seemed to look right back at her.

Duncan couldn't believe what he was seeing, he wasn't sure, but then Seherin looked away. Destiny lifted off and made her way to Duncan's side.

"Jamie," Duncan said, pushing his chair hard to catch up to his fleeing friend, "I think she can see Destiny."

"No, she can't," Jamie said. "She's not magic, she's crazy. If she saw a dragon, she'd have blamed me. You're worried about nothing. Stop seeing things that aren't there."

That's the problem. I see things that others think are not there…but they are.

Duncan inevitably recalled the words of the Hippogriff about being careful. Was this Ms. Seherin someone he needed to be worried about? Was she just a tough teacher who'd heard of some of the crazy things that happened last year? Or was she someone more dangerous?

Nothing was ever simple in this new role as Dragon Seeker, and it grew more complex every day.

Chapter 7   The First Test

With a mostly uneventful first week behind them, the school day took on a familiar rhythm. Arriving together in the morning, Duncan and Destiny met Jamie at the door.

Kathy came out of Templar's office. "I need to talk to you," she said, glancing at Jamie, "privately."

Jamie put up his hands in mock surrender. "Fine, fine, just kick the best friend to the curb. I can take a hint," wandering off down the hall.

"So, Duncan, how is the training going?" Mr. Templar said, joining Duncan and Kathy..

Duncan looked between the two. "With this sudden interest from you two, I have a feeling I am about to be put to some test."

"I told you," Kathy said, putting out her hand. Templar reached into his pocket, then handed her a five - dollar bill. Kathy waved it at Templar. "I knew he'd say that, never doubt me."

Templar motioned for them to move into the office.

"Okay, my boy, as Kathy predicted, and you surmised, costing me five dollars, we do have a task for you. One that will be a bit of a challenge, if Destiny is not ready for it."

At the sound of her name, Destiny materialized in front of them, dancing with excitement.

Templar stepped back, craning his neck to look at the dragon's head. "My, my you've grown. Pretty soon you won't fit inside here. What are you feeding her, Duncan?"

"Anything she wants, my parents are starting to think I am hoarding food or feeding the whole neighborhood. Although lately she's been foraging on her own. Every time I see one of those missing pet posters, I get nervous. And occasionally I see her drooling and eyeing Tripod, but so far nothing's happened."

Templar let out a laugh. "I don't think Destiny would do that, would you girl?"

Destiny ignored the question, avoiding looking him in the eye.

"No matter. I will arrange for a supply of food to be stored in the shed out behind the ball fields. No one uses that anymore and it will be out of sight so you can feed away in safety.

"We'll discuss things then, have a good day."
*****

Meeting after school in the woods near the ballfield, Templar, Kathy, and Duncan gathered away from inquisitive minds.

"Now on to our little task…" Templar said.

"You want me to what?" Duncan said, eyes wide open as the idea roiled his brain. 'And how am I supposed to do that?"

Templar smiled.

"Yeah, yeah," he held up his hands. "Figure it out, Duncan. You can do it, Duncan. Just tell the dragon what you want, Duncan. Like it's easy to just wave my hand

and say, Destiny, fly me to the top of the world and find Balinor..."

Before the last of his words drifted away in the air, Destiny scooped Duncan from his chair with front paws, placing him not so gently on her back, and stood ready to take off at Duncan's command. Duncan's wheelchair lay on its side.

Her quivering excitement bounced Duncan on her back.

"It would seem the training has gone fairly well," Templar said, chuckling as he stood the chair upright. "No time like the present to give it a try. What was the expression I once heard? Ah, yes, *today is a good day to die.*"

Duncan laughed. "Thanks, Mr. T, you always find the right thing to say."

Destiny pawed at the ground, short bursts of fire shot from her lips, bouncing side to side with anticipation.

Templar hooked Duncan's chair to a lanyard hanging around the dragon's neck and cinched it tight to her side. "Just in case you need it," he smiled, stepping back out of the way.

"Okay, Destiny, are you readyyyyyy...?" The last of the sentence was lost to the wind as the dragon leapt into the air. Duncan clutched tightly to the dragon's neck thinking the force of the Jetstream-like air would batter him.

But there was no such force, or even sound.

As they cleared the ground, Destiny spun back over Templar and Kathy, nearly knocking them to the ground.

"Hang on, Duncan," Kathy screamed as the pair rocketed off into the clouds.

Really? Duncan thought, gripping tighter, hang on? That would never have occurred to me. Hanging on so I won't die, how ingenious. Brilliant advice.

Glancing back over his shoulder he briefly glimpsed someone slinking along the edge of the trees surrounding the field where he'd left Kathy and Templar.

He couldn't be certain, but he had the sense they had curly blonde hair, or was it just the shadows of the trees? Or was it…?

He never had time to complete the thought. Destiny let out a roar disproportionally loud to her large yet still young body, flapped her wings, and the world went spiraling away from them.

Duncan saw the curve of the earth they were so high. The air was thin, silent, but he felt no chill. He knew he should be freezing this high up, and starving for oxygen, but he was not.

Destiny settled into a slow rhythmic pattern with her wings, and they glided through the air. For what seemed like hours, they soared high above the earth, Destiny sniffing the air and changing direction occasionally.

"I see you've trained her well, my old friend." The familiar voice of Balinor, the dragon who had been with him in the quest to find the hidden egg of the *LAST* dragon, enveloped him. Looking around, he saw nothing. Then, from out of the mists of a nearby cloud, a giant dragon emerged.

"Balinor, oh Balinor, it's so good to see you," Duncan said.

"And you as well, my boy. I see you've made great progress with the *LAST* Dragon."

"Destiny, her name is Destiny."

"So it is, Duncan, so it is. And as you are the Dragon Seeker, I should have known you would discover the name long before we met one last time."

Duncan's face took on a more serious look. "What do you mean, one last time?"

Balinor smiled as best a dragon could, then motioned for them to follow him. Swooping down through the clouds, they emerged over familiar ground, Diamond Hill in Cumberland, Rhode Island. Duncan's hometown, where much of this adventure began, and nearly ended.

"But why here?" Duncan asked as the two dragons came in to land, Balinor standing near him as he rested on Destiny's back.

"Life is a circle, my boy. Circles have no beginning or end, continuing forever, but we are just points in that circle. We live life. And then, in keeping with the rhythm of nature, we leave it to others. My time grows short. Your time, and Destiny's, are just beginning. Many challenges remain before the dragon is safely restored in the world. And how…no, if that happens, is all up to you two now, my part is finished."

"But I don't understand, Balinor, I thought…" his voice broke, and he couldn't go on.

"Remember when you would visit me in the secret cave along the Blackstone River? Remember what I said to you then in the old language?"

The words—strange, exotic, yet somehow familiar—came flooding back to Duncan. "'Se Draca álibbend, na des Draca…*The* dragon lives forever, but not *this* dragon."

Balinor smiled. "You've learned well, young Dragon Seeker. And so, my time is over."

Rising to his full height, towering over the smaller dragon and Duncan, Balinor smiled. "This is why Templar sent you here. So, you understand why it is important to protect those small dragons growing within Destiny, so the dragons may once again roam free.

"Dragons, and humans, are not immortal, but we carry within us immortal ideas. We love our family and friends, we defend them, we nurture them, and we protect them.

"In the past, some of our kind—both man and dragon—grew greedy and envious of things with no real value. Trinkets we fought over blinded us to the most important things.

"We followed a path away from the truth, and it cost us dearly. Life is not measured by what you've accumulated while you were alive, it is measured by what you've left behind for those who come after you in the circle of life.

"Remember that my good friend, and everything will be fine."

With one powerful thrust of his wings, Balinor powered away, disappearing into the noon sun, and was gone.

Duncan wiped a tear from his eye. He would miss his friend, but he would try to do what he asked.

I don't know why Mr. Templar sent me here. I didn't learn anything, and I can't see how this was a test.

"You've learned the most important thing," Destiny's words came to him in his thoughts. "You've learned why it is so important that we protect these young dragons and bring them to life. You've learned why this came to be and why we must do everything to restore the dragon to the world.

"And you have learned that all you went through before was preparing you for this moment. This was never meant to be a test where, if you passed, you got some special power to win out over evil.

"This was test designed to show you that you have all you need within you to accomplish what Balinor said is important in life, to leave something behind for those who come after you."

Destiny unfolded her wings, ready to fly, then paused a moment. "We will do this together, Duncan, and we will leave something behind that will last forever."

She took to the sky, spiraling to the edge of space, then dove back to earth.

Templar and Kathy, now joined by Jamie, stood in the same spot.

"You've been here waiting the whole time?" Duncan said, as he slid from the dragon and into his chair. His many flights with Balinor gave him lots of practice.

"You've only been gone five minutes, "Jamie said, "I watched you leave."

"That was you I saw sneaking along the tree line?"

Jamie looked confused, face scrunched up.

"Never mind. But how is that possible, I was gone for hours?" Duncan said, looking at Kathy.

She shrugged. "Time is apparently relative as I once read. A stubbornly persistent illusion."

That gave them all a laugh, except for Destiny who drooled on Jamie.

"Hey, watch it, yuck. Will you feed this thing?"

Duncan chuckled then pulled out a sandwich from his backpack, tossing it to the dragon. "It's a good thing that was not my favorite sandwich; I might not have been able to give it up so easily."

"Funny," Jamie said, "hysterical," as he wiped more slime from his head.

Templar pointed toward the school. "You two better get to class. Time might very well be an illusion, but I can't save you if you're late getting to class, it might bring too much attention to our collaboration. What kind of high school students hang around with the principal?"

Jamie chuckled. "You got that right, Mr. T. Who'd want to do that? Hang with some old guy."

Templar turned slowly around. "You know, on second thought, there might be just enough time to play one more round of fetch," he stared at Jamie. "This old guy loves that."

"Just kidding, Mr. T, just kidding. I love hanging with you. We're like besties."

"Yes, Mr. Haworth, my feeling exactly.

Chapter 8   Teacher Torture

"Misters Emeris and Haworth, late again I see," said Ms. Seherin as the two friends wheeled into the class. "Once again you shall be my guests for detention after school."

A round of snickers from the class drew the teacher's attention, her look alone froze silence them.

"But we were with Mr. Templar, "Jamie pleaded, "working on, a, working on a, a…"

"Working on what?" Seherin said, her eyes burning into Jamie's skull.

Duncan yanked on Jamie's sweatshirt.

"Ah, nothing, Ms. Seherin, nothing."

"I thought as much. Take your seats and let's hope you're prepared." She turned her attention to the whole class. "In light of this grand entrance, and since many of you found it amusing, we shall celebrate with a pop quiz. Books away, pens ready. Ten questions coming your way."

Duncan could feel the whole class staring at him, knowing they blamed him for the problem. Jamie was an airhead in their eyes, he knew better.

*****

Sitting in detention, Duncan amused himself by watching Destiny torturing Jamie. She would stay invisible until the last moment, then materialize and nip at him or knock his books off the desk, then fad away before anyone saw her. It drove Jamie to madness, but there was nothing he could do.

Ms. Seherin seemed not to notice, although Duncan was sure she saw something. I wonder if she is another Harper. Harper had been a teacher last year who pretended to be on their side while he searched for Dragon's egg.

But it turned out she was on the other side all along, the Raven Queen The Hippogriff warned me to be careful. I don't trust Seherin. I'm gonna talk to Templar about this.

Time seemed to drag. Duncan kept one eye on the clock and one eye on Ms. Seherin, praying for 3:00 P.M. bell and freedom.

Just two minutes to go, when Duncan noticed Destiny had lost interest in Jamie. Hovering just above the mostly empty desks, she seemed lost in thought. Then, as Duncan watched in horror, she swooped toward Seherin, knocking over her water bottle.

Startled by the cold water pouring onto her lap, she glanced up looking for a culprit.

Fortunately, Jamie and Duncan were too far away to be responsible, but still she eyed them. Grabbing paper towels from her desk, she wiped off her skirt and mopped up the puddle on the desk.

"You two, out," she said, pointing toward the door.

They didn't have to be told twice, grabbing their stuff, and moving fast. Destiny, unable to resist, flapped her wings sending the pile of papers scattering off the teacher's desk, then followed Duncan out the door.

"What are you trying to do, Destiny?" Duncan whispered through his gritted teeth. "You want us to spend every day in detention?"

Jamie laughed. "I thought it was funny, at least she left me alone."

Chapter 9   Keep Your Enemies Closer

"I have no reason to believe Ms. Seherin is anything more than what she appears to be," Templar said, "a teacher. Focus on the things that matter, Duncan, not some silly paranoid suspicions wafting around in your head. Or…" Templar spun to face Jamie, "or are these silly notions your doing, Mr. Haworth. They do seem to be your bailiwick."

"My what?" Jamie said, a confused look on his face.

"Never mind, my boy," Templar shook his head, "Never mind."

"So, Duncan are you ready for your birthing lessons?" Kathy said, smiling at the look on Duncan's face.

"Birthing lessons? What do you mean, birthing lessons?"

"You are a naïve one, aren't you?" Kathy smiled. "When Destiny is ready to lay her eggs, we have to help her," she put her hand on his shoulder, "and you will have the most important part."

Duncan's eyes narrowed, a frown on his face. "What kind of part?"

"You have to choose which one is the egg we will use to replace the one Destiny came from."

"Replace it, why? I thought that only happened in times of war?"

Kathy crossed her arms, staring at Duncan, waiting for the realization to kick in.

"Oh, yeah. To preserve the *LAST* dragon because we are in a war of sorts."

Kathy smiled. "You are pretty smart...for a boy."

Duncan tilted his head. "Thanks, I think. So now what?"

"First, we have to see how close Destiny is to being ready and then, oh yeah, one more thing."

"I'm almost afraid to ask."

"You have to name each egg." Kathy looked at Templar. "You want to tell him, or can I?"

"I would never deprive you of such pleasure," Templar bowed, flicking his hand for her to take the lead."

Duncan glanced at Jamie, then back at Templar and Kathy. "I've feeling I'm not going to like this."

"No shit, Sherlock," Jamie, whispered though his clenched teeth.

"I heard that, Mr. Haworth," Templar said, his look withering Jamie where he stood.

"Oops."

"Enough," Duncan interrupted, "just tell me how many. What, two? Three?"

"That would be a start, "Kathy said, "at least for the first day."

"The first day? What does that mean?"

Kathy hesitated for a moment, then moved closer to Duncan. Being so close to her always made Duncan feel special, but he knew she was just being kind. No doubt they were friends but anything else, was, well...unlikely.

"The egg laying process can take place over several days. In the beginning, two or three. By the end it could be fifty or hundred. Destiny might be different and lay them sooner, but we can know until it happens."

Duncan stared at Kathy, the reality of her words fighting against his sensibilities.

"Duncan? Duncan?" Kathy nudged his shoulder, then grasped his hand. A warmth flooded over him. Whatever she said no longer troubled him.

"Oh, okay," he smiled, although his eyes seemed to focus on something far in the distance.

"It would seem, my dear," Templar said, with a chuckle. "Your charms have eased the enormity of the task."

"Yeah," said Jamie, "that or he's just in love."

Kathy glared at him, then let go of Duncan's hand. The spell, or the moment, broken, Duncan came out of his trance.

"A hundred? I don't even know a hundred names. How am I supposed to think of so many names?"

Kathy smiled. "First things first, Duncan. Let's work on handling egg laying, then we can worry about names. Where's Destiny?"

Duncan looked past Kathy, "She's right over..." the words faded as the realization sunk in.

Destiny was gone...

Chapter 10   Unlikely Allies

"I told you we couldn't trust her," Jamie said, as they spotted Ms. Seherin headed toward the group. A coincidence, her showing up just as Destiny goes missing. I don't buy it" He started toward the teacher; more prelude to attack than welcome.

Duncan grabbed him by the sleeve, Jamie dragging him in his wheelchair a few feet before he relented.

"What are you doing?" he said, yanking himself away. "I'll find out what she did with her."

"Let's see what she has to say, Jamie. Think about it. If she's powerful enough to take a dragon without our knowing you aren't gonna get far threatening her."

"He's got a point, Jamie," Templar added. "I think you might be jumping to the wrong conclusion here. Let's see what she has to say first."

"Fine," Jamie said, glaring at the approaching Ms. Seherin. "But the minute she says anything that makes me think she's involved, I am gonna…"

"Gonna what, Mr. Haworth," Ms. Seherin said, "I've been looking for you two, once again."

Jamie said nothing, just stared at the ground.

"Mr. Templar, I require Mr. Haworth's help moving some books for my next section. Might I borrow him for a bit?"

"What about Duncan?" Jamie said, the words snarly and rough. "Trying to deny and conquer, are you?"

"What?" Seherin blinked several times, trying to fathom Jamie's demeanor. "I have no idea what you're talking about, but what I need is something you can do, and Mr. Emeris would be a bit challenged, under the circumstances."

Templar chuckled. "I think she means she needs brawn not brains, am I right, Ms. Seherin?"

"Exactly," she smiled. "I am an astute judge of capabilities. Since I noticed you standing here, I thought I would ask."

"What about Destiny?" Duncan said, "We need to find her."

"I wouldn't worry about her, my boy. She has some things to do on her own."

Chapter 11   A Labor of Fear

"Come along, Mr. Haworth," Ms. Seherin said. "I need you for a small task, I'm not leading you to your death."

I'm not so sure about that, Jamie thought as he shuffled along, uncertain of what lay ahead.

"You seem very protective of your friend Duncan, Mr. Jamieson," Seherin said as they walked down the hallway.

"What? Ah, well he is my friend and, well, because he's, ah…"

"Confined to a wheelchair?" Seherin finished the sentence for him,

"Yeah, that. I just like to keep an eye on him. Kids can be cruel."

"The whole world can be cruel, Mr. Jamieson. Having friends when you need them can make the difference between survival or demise. You'd do well to stay close to Mr. Emeris considering…" She let the end of the sentence drift off.

"Considering what?" Jamie asked.

Seherin smiled. "Let's just say you may find other friends in places you'd least expect."

Entering the classroom, Jamie spotted two large boxes of books.

"Those?" he pointed. "They look heavy."

"See, and I thought you were just simple," Seherin grinned. "Yes, they are heavy and that's why I needed help."

Jamie slid one of the boxes off the desk, almost dropping it. While the box was bulky and awkward, it wasn't quite as heavy as he feared. "Where do you want them?"

Seherin smiled. "Please take them to the back of the class near the door. That way everyone can select one on their way into class."

Jamie maneuvered the boxes to the back table. As he placed the last one, a small slip of paper fell from the box. Jamie looked up and Ms. Seherin was busy writing something on the board. Sliding the note with his foot from under the table, he bent down to grab it.

"Drop something, Mr. Haworth?" Seherin said, watching Jamie's movements.

"Nope, just tying my shoe," he said, hiding the note in his hand.

"Please move the other box, then you can return to whatever mischief you and your friend were up to."

Jamie hurried to move the other box as he slipped the note into his pocket. "All set, Ms. Seherin," he said over his shoulder as he ran out the door.

Finding a hidden alcove off the hall, he pulled the note from his pocket. When he read it, his heart almost leaped from his chest. I gotta find Duncan and Kathy. I knew that Seherin was trouble.

Chapter 12   Suspicions and Rumors

"It doesn't mean she's the enemy, Jamie," Duncan said, turning the note over in his hand. "But I suppose we do have to be careful."

"What?" Jamie said. "Did you read it? She is definitely the enemy."

"Duncan's right," Kathy said. "All this means is she suspects something is up, not plotting Duncan's demise."

Jamie snatched the note from Duncan's hand. He read it aloud. *D & J have Destiny for now.* Can't be any simpler than that. *For now!* She plans to steal Destiny and probably kill us."

Kathy glanced at Duncan, then shrugged. "Okay, okay. We'll keep an eye on her."

"How have you two survived without me?" Jamie asked. "If I weren't protecting you, you'd both be doomed."

Kathy laughed out loud. "If you're my protection, I am in trouble. Come on, let's go so I can start Duncan's birthing classes."

"Birthing classes?" Jamie said. "Ah, count me out. I'm gonna go keep watch on Seherin. I don't need to want anything to do with birthing dragons."

The two watched as Jamie took out his cell phone and started walking and texting.

"What are you doing?" Duncan asked. "I thought you were going to spy on Seherin."

"I am," Jamie smiled. "She'll never pay any attention to a teenager texting. It's the perfect cover, hiding in plain sight."

Duncan glanced at Kathy, who rolled her eyes. "You watch way too many cop shows, Jamie."

With Jamie off on his self-directed spying mission, Kathy looked to Duncan.

"Ready?"

"Aren't we going to find Destiny first?"

"No need, look," Kathy said, pointing to Jamie as he walked down the hall.

Destiny had reappeared and was matching Jamie step for step as he walked along.

"I wonder how long it will take the super spy to figure out she's right behind him?"

Duncan chuckled. "I'll give her one thing; she has a sense of humor."

"Okay, now that the disappearance has been solved, are you ready for your lesson in egg care?"

"Do I have a choice?"

"No, but I thought I'd at least give you hope. Come on, time you saw the special place."

"Isn't Destiny coming?"

"Oh, she'll be there, she's just taking a break from her latest task."

Pointing Duncan toward the woods surrounding the school, Kathy led the way down a winding path.

"Hey, I don't remember this path being here," Duncan said, bouncing his chair along the uneven but well-worn ground.

"Sometimes you don't see things because you aren't looking for them even when they're right in front of your eyes."

"What do ya mean?" Duncan said.

"I mean," Kathy answered, stepping aside so Duncan could see past her. "This." She held her right hand out, palm side up, and let Duncan take in the moment.

"What is that?" Duncan asked.

As the words came out, Destiny flew in carrying several large branches and a bundle of leaves.

"Is that a nest?"

"Wow, figured that out all by yourself, eh? Hope springs eternal."

"Funny, Kathy. But don't you think someone might find this? I mean the school is just through the woods…" As Duncan turned to point toward the school, he stopped talking.

"Ah, where are we? I should be able to see the school from here. What's going on?"

Kathy tilted her head and folded her arms, waiting for Duncan's brain to catch up.

"Never mind. Magic, I get it."

Destiny returned with another load of branches, dropping one branch that dug a hole in the ground close to Duncan. "Hey, watch it, Destiny. You almost hit me."

"What are you worried about?" Kathy said. "Ending up in a wheelchair?"

"Oh, you're on a real roll today, aren't you? So, this is where she'll lay her eggs?"

"Yup, and this is where you come in," Kathy pointed to the now giant nest.

"And how do you think I will get up there?" Duncan asked.

Hearing the words, Destiny's head popped over the rim of the nest.

"You're about to find out," Kathy said, a smile crossing her face.

In a flash, Destiny flew out of the nest, scooped Duncan out of his chair by the collar of his sweater and dropped him into the nest.

Duncan lay half seated half reclining in the soft concoction of tree limbs, branches, grass, and leaves.

"Ah, point of order," Duncan said. "How am I supposed to move in here? Even with my chair it would be impossible."

"Stand up," Kathy said.

"Are you nuts? Did she hit you with a branch? How am *I* supposed to stand up?"

Destiny bounced over and nudged Duncan with his snout.

"Hey, you're gonna..." And suddenly Duncan was standing. Or more accurately floating.

"What is going on?" Duncan said, moving ever so slightly forward, unaccustomed as he was to motion out of his chair.

Kathy smiled, now floating along with him.

"To add protection to the eggs, it has magic within. It cushions the eggs and allows us to move like this. An invisibility spell is also around the nest, hiding it from prying eyes. But here is the best part." And without another word, Kathy launched herself into the air, spinning round and round, then landing like a feather floating to the ground.

"Try it," she said.

"Me?"

"No, the other Duncan. Try it."

Duncan looked at Destiny, who was dancing with excitement even though she hovered a few feet over the nest.

"But my legs? How can I jump?"

"Believe, Duncan, believe," Kathy said.

And with that, Duncan closed his eyes and imagined himself jumping. When he opened his eyes, he was well above the rim of the nest.

"Holy cow, I can fly,' he yelled, spinning and twirling in the air. After a few moments, he settled back down. "That was wild."

Kathy smiled, then put her hand on his shoulder. "I know it was fun for you, but don't let it get out of control. This is all for the safety of the eggs. We need to go back to the real world, and you have to go back to your chair."

"But what about the birthing class?"

Kathy smiled, putting her hand on Duncan's shoulder as they lifted from the nest. With Duncan safely back in his chair, Kathy waved her hand, and the nest faded into nothingness.

Turning back to face him, she paused a moment. "I wanted to give you a few moments of fun before we have to get serious. Tomorrow, right after school. Meet me at the edge of the woods. Our work starts then."

Duncan turned to glimpse where the nest had been and when he turned back Kathy was gone.

Chapter 13   Our Worst Fear

"Gone?" Mr. Templar said, "What do you mean gone?"

"Gone, vanished, disappeared, fled the jurisdiction, no longer where she had been," Duncan said. "One moment she was right behind me and the next, gone."

"And this was after she showed you the nest?"

"Yeah."

"And Duncan, this is important, I need you to think about this. Was the nest still visible?"

"No, ah, I don't think so. Ah, no. I'm sure it wasn't."

Templar raised an eyebrow. "Are… you… sure?" he asked, spreading out the words.

"Yeah, I'm sure. After we left the nest and she put me back in my chair, I watched her wave her hand and the nest vanished."

Templar rubbed his eyes, pushing his horn-rimmed glasses up to his forehead. When he moved his hand, the glasses slipped down sitting cockeyed on his face. It was almost comical.

"Okay, then it is likely they didn't see the nest and will try to get Kathy to tell them where it is."

"Them? Who is them?" Duncan asked. "And how will they…"

"You don't want to know, my boy. Okay, go find Jamie, summon Destiny, then head to your house. Wait for me there."

"Where are you going?"

"To find out who took Kathy. Once I know who I will know where and figure out a way to get her back."

"No! I'm coming with you."

"Duncan, listen to me. You can't help. There are dangers you can't imagine, and you'll be at risk. I need to…"

The look on Duncan's face stopped Templar's words. Duncan was no longer the innocent boy who authored a story and revealed himself as something other than what he appeared.

Now he was the story and Templar knew to stand in his way was a mistake.

"Okay, my boy, time to face the worst of those who would destroy the dragons. Where is Jamie?"

Duncan shrugged.

"Well, get on that cellphone of yours and tell him to meet us here, now!"

Duncan reached for the phone, punched a few keys, and waited. A moment later, the phone started beeping.

Duncan read the message. "He wants to know why."

"Give me that blasted thing," Templar said, pushing the number to call Jamie, then putting it on speaker. "Why does this generation never just call someone instead of these idiotic texts?"

"Hey, who do you think you are?" Jamie's voice came through the phone. "You're not the boss of me, Duncan."

"Perhaps Duncan isn't, Mr. Haworth, but as long as I am the principal of this school, I am. Not unless you want to spend the next few centuries in a dark dungeon somewhere, which I can easily and gleefully arrange, I suggest you run, not walk, not stroll, *but run over here right now!*"

Templar clicked the phone off, handing it back.

"Is he on the way?" Duncan smiled.

Templar folded his arms. "He'd better be."

A moment later the sound of something crashing through the woods reached them, and a breathless Jamie came rushing from the trees.

"Fast enough, Mr. T?" He bent over, hands on his knees trying to catch his breath. Then ducking again as Destiny swooped in low and landed next to them.

"It'll do. I have a task for you."

"Wha…wha's…what's that?" the still breathless Jamie asked.

"Get in the nest," Templar said.

"Nest? What nest?" Jamie asked, looking around as his breathing eased. "I don't see any nest."

"This one," Templar said, waving his hand.

"What the…? Oops, sorry Mr. T. I should know by now not to be surprised by anything that happens around here."

Jamie walked around the nest, craning his neck to see over the edge which was too high. Destiny hopped in.

"How am I supposed to get…" As the words left his mouth, Destiny popped over the side, reached down, and hauled him by the hood of his sweatshirt.

"Hey," Jamie yelled, "you can't leave me here alone with this thing. What if she gets hungry?"

"Then you won't be alone anymore, will you?" Templar said.

"Thanks, Mr. T, that's comforting," Jamie said, backing away from the dragon.

"Watch this," Templar whispered to Duncan out of the corner of his mouth. "Destiny, play ball."

The sound of Jamie protesting as he appeared bouncing up and down, in and out of view, echoed as Destiny played a one-sided game of catch.

"Make……her……stop……please," Jamie said, one word at a time as he came into view.

"Mr. T, I think that's enough," Duncan said. "If she keeps that up, he may barf all over the place."

Templar smiled. "You're right, my boy. I just couldn't resist. Destiny, stop!"

Jamie appeared one last time, pasty, grasping the top of the nest, Destiny mere inches behind him poised to start the game again.

"Now will you tell me why I am in here playing the part of a dragon's toy?"

"Of course, we have to go find Kathy and…"

"Kathy?" Jamie interrupted, suddenly seeming quite serious and less nauseous. "Has something happened to her? Is Seherin involved? I knew we shouldn't trust her. Where is she?"

"Jamie, if you give me a moment, I'll explain."

"Okay, but if Seherin did anything…"

"Yes, yes, you unleash your considerable powers against her. I'm sure she'll be terrified. But I doubt it is her anyway. Whoever took Kathy must be very powerful. She is not an easy target. As I was trying to tell you, once I know who took her, I will know where to look.

"Your job is simple, that's why I knew you'd be perfect. We will hide the nest again. All you have to do is listen and watch for anyone who may come to look for it. You'll be able to see and hear them, but you and the nest will be invisible to them. Got it?"

"And if I see someone, what do I do? Have Destiny eat them?"

"No, no, nothing so dramatic. Use that cellphone of yours that rarely leaves your hands and shoot pictures. We need to know who or what we are facing before we decide how to act."

"Okay, Mr. T, I can do that."

"One other thing, Jamie," Templar said, glancing around.

"What?"

"I am assuming they haven't found the nest. If I am right, they'll just come back to try again. But if I'm wrong…"

"Wrong? How do you mean, wrong?"

"If they have found the nest, they will try to uncloak it. That may not be a pleasant experience. You see, they prefer to capture Destiny and the nest. But failing that, well, destroying it, and anything or anyone in it would be almost as good for their purposes."

Jamie looked at Duncan and then back at Templar. Destiny came to his side, nuzzling against him.

Pushing himself up higher on the edge of the nest, Jamie swung his legs around to sit facing out. He scratched Destiny's head as the dragon softly purred.

"You go find Kathy; I'll stay here no matter what happens."

"Jamie," Templar said, "you are a remarkable young man once you get past the deceptive surface."

"Thanks, I think," Jamie said, and started patrolling around the rim of the nest, enjoying the relaxed gravity, as it faded from view.

Chapter 14   Where To Look?

"Where do we start?" Duncan asked as they walked out of the woods. Templar ignored the question, studying the ground around them.

"There!" Templar pointed, "I should have known."

Duncan tried to follow Templar's eyes but could see nothing. "I don't see anything."

"Don't just use your eyes. Use your experiences with magical creatures. Look at things not as Duncan Emeris but as the Dragon Seeker. How do you think these beings have survived so long without anyone detecting them? Look, Duncan, look at things differently."

Duncan stared at the ground, trying to imagine what kind of a creature might overcome Kathy. He saw nothing. "I don't see anything, Mr. T, how am I supposed to help her."

Templar raised his eyebrows. "Remember what Kathy said about seeing with all your senses."

Duncan closed his eyes, took a deep breath, and then slowly opened them. At first nothing, but then he sensed it. A shimmering in the air like a mirage. Fleeting, flickering in and out of view, like viewing something through ripples in water.

"I see it. I see it!" he said, recognizing the signs of a magic trail.

"Good, good, my boy. No tell me, what kind of a creature would make that trail?"

"I'm not sure, something small, I think. But how could something so small take Kathy?"

"Remember it's not the size of the wand but the magician behind it," Templar said.

"So, they have powerful magic?"

"Indeed, and now I know where we need to look."

"Where does a creature like this hide?" Duncan asked.

"They don't," Templar said. "They just blend in among us."

"So, Jamie is right? Seherin is behind this?"

"No," Templar chuckled. "She is not behind this. I'm not saying we can just ignore her, but she isn't responsible for this."

"Okay, so now what?"

"Now we go back to the school and visit the library. Come on."

The two headed off following the now fading trail.

"The library?" Duncan asked. "Why there?"

"Because that's where we will find Kathy."

"In the library? Wouldn't someone notice a person being held prisoner? The place is not that big."

"Not if they've hidden her in the past."

"The past? Like in time travel? I thought that was impossible."

Templar stopped in his tracks. "Says the boy in a wheelchair who has ridden on dragons, battled wizards and mythical creatures, and is about to restore the dragons to the world."

"Oh yeah, there is that. But I still don't get it. What kind of creatures are these?"

"Time travelers. But with specific purposes. They aren't random. They've been sent ahead in the future in case they're needed. They come with a particular skill. Some are just spies. Some can manipulate beings. And some, the most dangerous, can slip back and forth in time, taking others with them.

"I suspect Kathy thought she had no alternative but to go with them because they threatened you. She likely knew it was an empty threat—they need you to control Destiny and the eggs—but she gambled she could buy enough time for us to figure it out and get to her. They'll try to get her to reveal the location of the nest. She won't, no matter what they do, but I don't want her to endure any more than she has to."

"Endure?" Duncan said.

"Don't go there, come on. If I remember correctly these creatures cannot function long without returning to their own time. My guess is they've stashed Kathy within the pages of some obscure book and will come back for her later."

"In a book? How do they do that?" Duncan asked.

"These beings are just ideas, concepts, descriptive narratives that magic brings to life. They turn her into a word or sentence or paragraph depending on how powerful she is and embed her in the text.

"Knowing what Kathy is capable of she will not have gone easily. She'll be hidden, but there will be something unnatural about the language. The challenge is how to narrow it down to one or two books. And one other problem."

"Now what?" Duncan asked.

"Others will come looking for the nest. I hope Jamie can keep his wits about him and just observe."

"Ah, Mr. T, do you really want to use the term," making the air quote motion, "keep his wits and Jamie in the same sentence?"

"Good point, all we can do is hope."

As they made their way into the library, the librarian greeted them.

"What brings you in, Mr. Templar? Does Duncan need something special? I'd be happy to help. We get so few unplanned visitors these days."

"No, no, Ms. Johnson. Duncan and I will just be browsing. I'm trying to encourage more use of the materials here. We'll be fine."

They both watched the librarian hesitate for a moment, then return to her office where she kept a wary eye on them.

"You don't think…" Duncan said, glancing between Templar and Ms. Johnson.

Templar shook his head. "No. I've known her for nigh on three decades. She's no more magical than most of the students in this school. She's just protective of her library material."

A noise drew their attention to a nearby bookshelf with a sign reading, *Reserved Please See Librarian* on it. A book called *The Land of Opposites* had fallen to the ground.

"Hmm," Templar said. "I wonder..." He opened the book and flipped through the pages. "No, too obvious." He pushed the book back in its place and turned to Duncan. The book popped off the shelf again.

The two looked at each other. The Duncan spun his chair and went to the opposite side of the room. A jumble of books in no special order sat on the shelves. As he started to reach for a book, the librarian was at his side.

"No, no, Duncan, those books are already reserved. If you need one of those titles I can put you on the waiting list."

"I don't want to check them out, I just wanted to look at them."

The librarian shook her head. "I've placed them in a particular order, and I don't want you meddling with them, thank you very much."

Templar came over and tapped Ms. Johnson on the shoulder. As she turned around, Templar motioned with his eyes for Duncan to make his move.

Slowly moving his chair to get behind the now agitated librarian, she was raving about people not following the rules, Duncan reached for one book and slid it behind his back.

"I understand, Ms. Johnson. No, no, Duncan and I will look elsewhere for something of interest. Sorry to trouble you."

Ms. Johnson spun around, eyeing first the bookshelf and then Duncan. "Well, no harm I suppose. I guess I should be thrilled that a student is so interested in a real book instead of those blasted digital things. How anyone can enjoy reading without the feeling of a book in their hands I'll never understand..."

"Yes, yes, Ms. Johnson, I agree. Sorry to trouble you. Come on, Duncan, I have a book in my office you might find quite interesting."

Fleeing from the library, they made their way to an empty hallway.

"What did you see, my boy?"

"This," Duncan said, reaching behind and pulling out the book.

"The Lord of the Rings?" Templar asked. "A bit obvious don't you think?"

"That's the point, Mr. T. It's what they wanted us to think."

Templar rubbed his chin. "Ah, a disinformation campaign, I see. How did you know?"

"I didn't until that book fell off the shelf. I bet Kathy managed to put some sort of spell on it knowing we'd come looking. She must have suspected they try to hide her in plain sight hoping we'd miss it."

"You know, Duncan, at this rate you won't be needing my help much longer."

"I doubt that Mr. T." A moment later the book fell off Duncan's chair and hit Templar on his foot.

"Hmm, I think you've just been proven correct. Kathy wants out. But now comes the hard part. How do we do this without causing her any permanent damage."

"Damage?" Duncan asked.

"Yeah, a side effect of her imprisonment. She is now bound within the book. They've made her part of the story. If we aren't careful in breaking the magic, she could be injured or worse."

"Can't you just reverse the spell?"

"Not so easy, I'm afraid. We need help with this one."

"What kind of help?"

"Keladry, my boy. She's the only one I can think of who is clever enough to solve this dilemma. Problem is I am not sure where to find her."

"What do we do?"

"First, let's get back and check on Jamie. You two are already being hunted down by whosever's class you're missing right now. You'll just have to endure some additional detention I suppose, but all for a good cause."

"Yeah, tell Jamie that. It's Seherin's class and we all know how Jamie feels about her."

Duncan wheeled around and headed toward the woods.

Chapter 15   In the Most Unexpected Places

"Detention? For what?" Jamie protested. "If I recall correctly, Mr. T, you told me to stay here with Destiny. I was on my way to class when you made me come here."

"I'm sure you were, Mr. Haworth, but we've no choice. Unless you want to explain to Ms. Seherin how you missed class to guard an invisible nest and protect a dragon."

Jamie paused for a moment, then a smile crawled across his face. "Well, when you put it that way. But I better not have to do this again."

Templar and Duncan both stared at Jamie.

"Fine, I know, I know. I'll be spending my life in detention just because I decided to be Duncan's friend."

"Yeah," Duncan said, "but without me, you'd still be in second grade."

"Yeah, right. Now tell me where Kathy is and how we can get her back."

Duncan held up the book. "She's in here."

Jamie squinted his eyes. "In a book? How'd she end up in a book?"

Templar tapped his temple.

"Oh, yeah," Jamie said, "magic, of course. So, wave your wand and set her free."

"Not that simple I'm afraid," Templar said. "We need to find Keladry."

"Keladry, why?"

"Because this is something she is better at than me," Templar said, holding his hand in front of Jamie. "And do not say a word, Mr. Haworth. Duncan, give me the book. You two head back to school and come to my office after you spend a pleasant hour with Ms. Seherin absolving your sins.

"Meanwhile, I'll try to figure out where to find Keladry."

Two hours later, Duncan rolled into Templar's office.

"Where's Jamie?" Templar asked.

"Ms. Seherin said she had some project she needed help on and made Jamie stay behind. She said it wouldn't take long and told me to leave."

"Hmm, I'm starting to wonder if Jamie's suspicions of her are well placed. Ah, well no matter. On to our bigger problem, finding Keladry."

"Wait, should we be worried about Jamie?"

"Worried, no. Terrified for his survival, perhaps." Templar tried but couldn't suppress his smile.

"I heard that, Mr. T," Jamie said, walking into the room.

"See, Duncan, nothing to worry about," Templar said.

"Yeah, thanks Mr. T. Look, I am telling you there's something weird about Seherin. She asked me to stay, made me move one box, then told me to leave. Anyone could have moved that box. Why'd she want me to stay?"

"I have no idea, Jamie. But I think you're right to be concerned. Steer clear of her whenever you can."

"Did you find Keladry?" Duncan asked.

"Ah, yes and no," Templar answered.

"Yes, and no? What does that mean?"

"Yes, I believe I know where she is. No, I am not certain trying is a smart move."

"Why not?" Duncan asked. "If she's the only one who can free Kathy what other choice do we have?"

"Well, here's the thing, Duncan. To get to Keladry someone needs to make a long journey. One that has no guarantee of success."

"I don't care what it takes," Duncan said, "Tell me where this is, and Destiny and I will go."

"Yes, well, it's not *where* you have to go, it's *when*."

"When? That doesn't make any sense. We can't wait. I need to go now."

"No, no, my boy," Templar said, putting his hand on Duncan's shoulder. "Of course we have to do this now. The problem is I know where she is, but not where she is *in a particular time*."

"Time travel?" Jamie said. "But that's not possible, I mean, not really possible, is it?"

"If you've learned anything these last few months, Jamie, it should be that little is impossible once you set your mind to it."

"You're right, Mr. T. Okay, tell us where, or when, and Duncan and I will go get her."

Templar stared at the two friends, their youthful enthusiasm making them certain of their invincibility.

"He can't come with me, can he?" Duncan said.

"What?" Jamie said, moving to stand next to Duncan. "No way. NO WAY I am gonna let my friend go off by himself. Not happening, Mr. T. I don't care what is out there, I'm going." He folded his arms and forced a determined look on his face.

"You're right, Jamie, you are going. It's Duncan who can't go."

Jamie slumped. "Huh?"

"No way, Mr. T," Duncan said. "Jamie has no magic. I barely know what I'm doing. You can't send him alone."

"No, Duncan. I can't send him. He needs to volunteer." He held up his hand stopping Jamie from speaking. "But before you let your bravado overwhelm your common sense, listen. This will not be easy. There's a very good chance you won't make it back unhurt, if at all. You need to consider this carefully.

"I can give you some advice and guidance, but you'll be on your own."

"Why can't Duncan go with me?" Jamie asked, the certainty of a moment ago fleeing in the face of the unknown.

"Magic," Templar said. "Where Keladry exists are myriad magical creatures and beings. They are sensitive to other magical creatures. They would sense Duncan as soon as he arrived and plot to capture him, preventing him from returning to our time. We cannot have that. The dragon must endure, and Duncan is the only one who can insure this.

"Listen, we all want Kathy back but whatever compelled her to go with these creatures must have been powerful. She knew what she risked and did it anyway. It may be there is no way to get her back, and she would've known that.

"I can't make the decision for you; you must do this in your own accord. But remember this, as hard as it may be, all of us are expendable if it protects the return of the dragon. We all knew that, Kathy, Keladry, Duncan, and I when we assumed the mantle.

"This is not your quest. You're in this because Duncan is your friend, and we all respect that. You have no obligation to risk yourself for any of us. You've already done more than any of us could imagine."

Jamie glanced at Duncan, then back at Templar. Taking a deep breath, he tried to calm the gnawing fear.

"Mr. T, you already know my answer. Duncan isn't just a friend; he is my best friend. There is nothing or no one, magical or otherwise, that I wouldn't face for him. Tell me what I have to do, and I promise I will be back."

"You sure, my boy?"

"I am, let's do this."

Templar looked at Duncan. "Anything you want to say?"

Duncan shook his head. "He's as stubborn as they come. I couldn't talk him out of it even if I had a month." He rolled forward, reaching out to fist bump Jamie. "Come back, buddy, okay?"

"I will, who else is gonna put up with pushing your butt all over the place?" He forced a smile, then turned to Templar. "Ready for duty, your majesty."

Templar bent down and whispered in Jamie's ear. Duncan watched as his friend's eyes grew wider and wider.

"Really?"

"Really," nodded Templar. "Ready?"

"As I'll ever be," he said, stepping back. "Wait, wait."

"Change your mind?" Templar said.

"No, no, I'm going. Hey Duncan, if I don't get back, you can have my bike," a smile broke out on his face. "Oh wait, never mind," and in a flash, he disappeared.

"Always the smartass," Duncan said.

"Indeed, Duncan," Templar said. "But I will miss that smartass if…" he left the words hanging, the dread unspoken.

Duncan glanced one more time at the spot where Jamie once stood. Be safe, my friend, he thought, then something popped into his head. I wonder…

Chapter 16   The Land Time Keeps Hidden

It took a moment for Jamie to orient himself. Some things looked familiar, the trees, Diamond Hill off in the distance, the canal along the Blackstone River. But this was not the Cumberland of his time. The sounds, the smells, even the temperature felt different.

Jamie looked down and felt the ground shaking beneath his feet. A rhythmic pounding that shook everything. Looking to the other side of the river, Jamie could see the tops of trees shaking and rattling. Something was moving them. Something large. Something he preferred to avoid meeting.

Moving behind a vine-covered stone wall, the cool rocks damp and slimy to the touch, Jamie peered over the top. He had to shake his head, then rub his eyes before he could consider what appeared before him.

A dragon, enormous, red scaled, wings the size of an airplane, lumbered into view. And he could tell something else about the creature. It was hunting. Sniffing the air in one direction, then another. It had the scent but not the direction. He watched the dragon take an enormous deep breath, then looked right to where Jamie was hiding.

Didn't Mr. T say not being magic would keep the magical ones from sensing me. Jamie thought. Yeah, right. I should have taken a shower before I came here. Time to move.

Crawling along the wall, Jamie would pop his head up every few seconds to make sure the dragon hadn't spotted him. So far, so good. But Jamie wasn't taking any chances.

Ducking back behind the wall, he crawled a few more feet, soon reaching the end. A gap of a hundred yards loomed from where the wall ended to where the forest offered refuge, but this posed a challenge. If he could make it there, he'd be safe. If not, dragon food.

But it was still the length of a football field, and a good reason he spent his whole football career on the bench. He was *not* a fast runner. The coach, seventy-two years old when Jamie tried out, said *his mother*, ninety-three, was faster.

If the dragon spotted him, there's no way he'd make it. He'd seen dragons fly. They were anything but slow. But he couldn't stay here; sooner or later the dragon would catch his scent and find him.

Running, he thought, was his only choice.

'No, it's not," a voice said. Jamie let out a gasp, then covered his mouth.

"Don't run, walk," the voice added.

Jamie looked around, he saw no one. "Who, who are you? Where are you?"

"Here, right here. Look down."

Jamie looked at the ground and was surprised to see a tiny field mouse looking back.

"You want me to take advice from a mouse?" Jamie asked.

"Well, you are talking to one, aren't you? Remember where you are."

"Hmm, good point. Why should I walk?"

"Because that dragon can't see very well. He hunts by smell only to get near his prey. What happens then is panic sets in. The prey runs and the dragon senses the movement. If you walk, taking one step after another without panic, he can't see you.

"It's in their scales. They can feel the movement in the air. It's how they fly so well."

"Ah, that almost makes sense," Jamie said, glancing back at the dragon. "But still…"

"Look Jamie, we need to get out of here if your gonna find Keladry."

"You know my name?"

"Duh, you think Templar would send you, *you*, here to fend for yourself?"

"Yeah, good point. He said something about allies."

"We knew you'd be coming so we were watching."

"We?"

"The mice. We're everywhere, you know. Always have been, always will be."

"Okay, ah what do I call you?"

"Well, my formal name is M4253859373527101038392. But you can call me Miles."

"Huh, that's quite the name, Miles."

"Yeah, every mouse has a number name. It's how we know which family we come from. I'm the 42 branch."

"Ah, the meaning of life," Jamie said, a smile on his face.

"What?" asked Miles.

"Never mind." Jamie glanced over the wall and saw the dragon wading across the river like it was a puddle. "I think it's time we test your theory."

Miles scampered to the top of the wall. "Yup, an excellent time. Okay, just walk like I said. Once you start, don't stop, just keep going."

Jamie hesitated, then lifted his head. He pulled himself up, glanced back at the dragon, then took one step toward the woods.

The dragon stopped mid-river and sniffed the air.

Another step.

Another sniff.

Another step.

Another sniff.

Another step.

Another sniff.

And the dragon's eyes locked on him.

"Oops," Miles said. "This one is different, RUN!"

Jamie glanced at the mouse, then took off. Had the coach seen this he'd have been on the starting team.

They made the forest just as the dragon climbed the bank. Rising into the air, the dragon circled above. They knew what was next.

"Now what?" Jamie asked. "Any more brilliant mouse wisdom?"

Miles glanced at Jamie, then back at the dragon. The smoke was now rising from its snout as the dragon readied the attack.

"Back to the water, now. Crawl as fast as you can. The water is deep here, and it will protect you. Just stay close to the edge of the bank."

"Where are you going?"

"Underground, deep. Don't worry, I'll find you, if you're not a pile of ash. Now go."

Jamie made it to the bank and slipped into the water just as the firestorm enveloped the spot they'd been standing on a moment ago. Jamie watched as the dragon made several passes, igniting everything.

The water was freezing, but it was better than being turned to soot. He hadn't been here more than twenty minutes and already he almost died. And his one ally was a mouse.

This was not going well. How was he ever going to find Keladry? Never mind that, how was he ever going to survive?

It seemed like hours before he heard Miles calling him.

"Over here," Jamie said, crawling onto the bank. "I don't suppose you have dry clothes that will fit me, do you?" Muddy and shivering, he stood looking down on Miles.

"No, but I do know where we can go to get you warm and dry. Follow me." And with that, the mouse ran off.

Now, if you've ever tried to follow a mouse you know it is almost impossible. Miles kept circling back to guide Jamie along, pointing the way with his tail.

"Why don't you just walk so I can keep up with you?"

"Mice never walk, particularly when a cat or dragon is nearby. We run to live another day." Miles ran around in a few circles, pointed with his tail, and took off again.

Yeah, I noticed, Jamie thought, then tried to keep up.

After what seemed like forever, Jamie could see a glowing, shimmering light ahead.

"What's that?" he asked as Miles returned to check on him.

"The house of a friend," Miles said. Adding "I hope," just under his breath.

"You hope? What does that mean?"

"It means," came an unfamiliar and not the least bit comforting voice, "that despite my specific warning not to bring the unmagical here, Miles here has done just that. And managed to make a bit of an enemy of the local Red Dragon. Haven't you, Miles?"

Miles ran up Jamie's leg and perched on his shoulder. "Well, you see, Damien, it's like this…"

Damien put his hand out, placing his thumb and fingers together. Miles fell silent.

"Tell me why I shouldn't let my cats play with you for a bit and then enjoy tearing you apart for dinner?"

Jamie stepped forward. "Hey, pal, I don't know who you are, but Miles here saved my life. You try to feed him to some mangy cat, you and I are gonna have a problem."

A grin crossed Damien's face. "My, my, an unmagical being with a sense of honor. Who knew such a thing existed?" He studied Jamie.

"Now, now, young man, need for such bravado. While I prefer not to associate with beings such as you, thus my isolation here in this time, I know *why* Miles brought you here.

"The question is," he rubbed his chin, "can I help you and, if so, how will that happen? I need to consider the options." He turned, waving his arm toward the path. "Come with me while I consider this. There's a fire and I think you might be a bit hypothermic."

"No," Jamie shook his head. "I'm just really cold."

Damien rubbed his chin. "And Myrrdin picked *you* for this task, did he? Hmm…interesting choice."

Chapter 17   The Greater Good

Warmed by the fire and wearing comfortable, if unconventional, attire that made him look like he'd walked out of a Shakespearean play, Jamie watched Damien pace back and forth.

"What is he doing?" Jamie asked.

"Thinking, I think," said Miles, scampering from Jamie's shoulder and snatching a crumb of cheese he'd spotted near the fireplace.

"Thinking about what?"

"One of two things. One, how to help us. Two, how to get rid of us," Mile answered, whiskers flicking back and forth in search of any encroaching cats.

"I thought you said he was a friend."

"Well, by friend, I meant someone I wasn't certain of his reaction. The others I know would have just fed us to the dragon."

"Great," Jamie said.

"This Keladry creature you're so intent on finding, she is important to you?" Damien said, breaking his silence.

"Well, she is my friend. But it's not for me. We have another friend who's been imprisoned in a book. Mr. T, ah, Mr. Templar, says she's the only one who can free her."

"I see," Damien said. "I must say this surprisingly selfless behavior by someone like yourself is contrary to all my prior experience with humans. Altruism is not your strong suit."

"All true what?" Jamie said.

"Altru…never mind. In a book you say? Was this during a session with your dragon?"

"You know about Destiny?"

Damien nodded. "All that nonsense between the dragons and others is precisely why I came here. To avoid that entanglement. But I see I cannot avoid it. I will help you. But I must warn you, this will not be easy."

Jamie glanced at Miles. "Doesn't matter, I came to get her, and I will do whatever it takes."

Damien stepped closer, then put his hand on Jamie's shoulder. "Does that include being trapped here in this time forever, young man? Because in dealing with those with such power it is as likely an outcome as any other. Perhaps more."

Jamie took a deep breath. "I said anything, and I meant it."

"And courage, too," Damien said. "Will wonders never cease? Okay, here's the plan, such as it is."

Chapter 18   The Best Laid Plans…

"What did you say these creatures are called?" Jamie whispered, peeking over the edge of the cliff.

"They are called many things by different creatures," Damien said. "They've existed since the beginning of the ages. I know them as the Psion. They steal the destiny of other creatures."

"How do you steal someone's destiny?" Jamie asked.

"By taking something or someone they need to fulfill it. It would seem, young human, that someone is you."

"Me? Then why did they put Kathy in the book?"

"Because you are necessary to her destiny. Believe it or not, she needs you to help Duncan return the dragon to the world."

Jamie thought for a moment, then the light came on. They knew Templar would send me! This whole thing is a trap. As the idea registered in his brain, something else alarmed him.

"Hey, where's Miles?" he asked, glancing around for the mouse.

"By now," Damien said, "I imagine my cats are digesting him." He was on Jamie in a flash, ensnaring him with a powerful spell.

"Hey, what the…? Let me go." Jamie said, struggling against bonds he could not see.

"All in good time, my simple friend. All in good time." Waving his hand, he lifted Jamie into the air and headed off into the den of the Psion.

As they made their way inside, the Psion surrounded Jamie. They didn't speak but hissed in a continuous chorus.

"Yes, yes," Damien said. "I'm certain he was alone. Miles will no longer trouble you. Now, I've kept my part of the bargain. Leave me out of this nonsense."

Jamie watched as Damien left the den, disappearing back into the forest.

One of the Psion slithered over, looking him up and down. At first, it was just more hissing noises, unintelligible sounds. But then a voice emerged.

"What manner of creature are you? Wizard, acolyte, or familiar?"

"I'm Jamie, a kid. But I'm gonna kick your ass if you don't let me go."

The Psion hissed more, then continued. "Even a creature as ignorant as you can see the obvious, you are in no position to threaten us.

"But here's your one chance to survive. Bring us this Dragon Seeker, and we will let you live. Refuse and dying will be your only relief from the agony. And you will wish it to come sooner…"

Jamie started to speak but stopped when he saw the light growing brighter in the back of the lair. Soon, an image appeared within the light. Fuzzy at first, then growing more defined.

"Recognize anyone?" the Psion asked.

Jamie squinted, then his heart began to race. Keladry, now visible, appeared suspended in a cage over what looked like a volcano. Jamie recognized it from the one book series he enjoyed reading. Mt. Doom from Lord of the Rings.

When Keladry saw Jamie, she cried out. "Don't listen to them, Jamie!" Her voice went silent while her lips still moved.

"Oh, did I forget to mention we'll make you watch your friend go first. Just so you know you cannot resist."

Jamie struggled against the invisible restraints but gave up. Force was not an option here. This required him to think. Maybe Mr. T made a mistake, he thought, I'm not exactly the intellectual type.

"Oh, but you are, Jamie, "a voice at once familiar yet unrecognized whispered. He looked around, but there was no one except the Psion.

"Looking for a way out?" the Psion hissed. "There is none."

The Psion was right, but he'd also given Jamie information. They didn't hear the voice. It must be all in my head. Hmm, that might be a problem, he thought.

"Jamie, I can help you," the voice said.

"Who are you?"

"A friend of Duncan. He thought you might need help."

"Great, get me out of this, this, spell or whatever it is."

"That I can't do."

"Hmm, didn't you say you were here to help? What can you do, offer encouragement?"

"That, in a manner of speaking, is exactly what I can do. You need to think your way out of this."

Jamie shook his head then, eyeing the Psion watching him, had a thought.

"So, if you want me to bring Duncan here how do you expect me to do that if I am held prisoner?"

"Smart, Jamie," the voice said. "Using your head."

"Oh, that is simple," came the hissing answer. "We will send you back, not alone of course, one of us will be watching, but you will go back and bring Duncan to the place we choose.

"Once he is in our grasp, you will be free to live your pathetic life."

"And Keladry?"

"What is she to you?"

"My friend."

The Psion made a sound like laughter. "So is the Dragon Seeker, but you'd give him up to save your own life. Why bother about her?"

Jamie was at a loss.

"Think Jamie, think," whispered the voice.

"Look, I can't do anything about Duncan. He's the Dragon Seeker. Maybe he'll prove to be more trouble than you imagine. But that is beyond my control. I *can* save Keladry. Although…"

"Although what?"

"How can I trust you to release her?"

"A dilemma indeed. I suppose you can't, but she *will* die if you refuse, so you'll have to take the chance."

Jamie considered the options. Duncan was the prize. Kathy, Keladry, and I are just the means to the end. They'd have no need once they had Duncan. They'd have no reason to abide by the bargain either, but that was also out of his hands.

I bet Mr. T and Duncan knew this all along and saw no other way. Well, Mr. T did. Duncan would never let me come here alone if he knew.

"Jamie," the voice said, "now you're thinking like a true begging dragon warrior."

"Warrior? I'm no warrior. What I am is pissed, and one way or the other, I will find a way to keep Duncan safe."

"So, what's it gonna be, human? You going to watch your friend die and then suffer at our hands begging for death, or are you gonna do as we ask?"

Jamie put out his hands. "Let me go. I'll find my own way back."

The Psion smiled, as if such a thing possible with these beings. "I think not. I will be with you the whole way. One false move and your friend, and you, will cease to exist."

With a wave of his hand, Jamie's bonds fell away. Rubbing his wrists, he had to fight the urge to charge the Psion. But he knew it would be useless. Something about coming with me was a hint. They said watching me. I wonder…

Chapter 19   Double Cross

With no other options, Jamie walked out of the lair and looked around. The last thing Mr. T said to him was that the way home will always be right in front of you. Why he spoke in riddles, I'll never understand, Jamie thought. Must be a teacher thing.

No time for ideal thoughts. Right in front of me, what did that mean?

Right in front of me.

"Something wrong?" the Psion hissed, now appearing as a more solid yet still shimmering mirage.

"Nope, just planning my departure."

"Well, be quick about it, or I'll make you pick which friend should die first."

Hmm, Jamie thought, this Psion has no idea how to go back. He *needs* me to take him. He wants me to believe he is in control, but he is not. Something isn't right here. Why would a creature with such power here need me to take him back to our time?

And then it dawned on him. Maybe this was all a ruse. A trick. Maybe they didn't have Keladry. They just want us to believe it.

But what if I'm wrong? What if they have her? How did I get into this mess? Okay, man, nothing I can do but figure it out as I go along.

First, I need to get back to my time. Then, I'll think of something to trap this creature in his own game.

"Ready?" Jamie asked.

"Let's go, no tricks or your friend will be ashes."

Jamie looked around, then saw Miles scampering back and forth trying to get his attention. He was trying to tell him something. Follow him! He wanted Jamie to follow.

I guess this is where I make it up as I go along, Jamie thought.

"Come on, this way," he said, walking toward Miles and hoping the Psion didn't notice.

As they made their way to the river, Miles pointed to the water. Oh man, not swimming again. The water is freezing. Jamie started down the bank.

"Where are you going?" the Psion hissed.

"Across the river, to the portal back to my time."

"Find another way," the Psion said. "There must be another way."

And then Jamie knew what he had to do. Something he had read in one of Duncan's stories about such creatures. Something he thought Duncan made up before all this Dragon Seeker stuff started. Now, he knew it was the answer to saving his friend.

"There is none. No bridge for miles. We have no choice," he watched as the apparition turned into solid form. "If you can't swim, I can carry you across. It's not over my head."

Jamie sensed the creature's hesitation, it all made sense now. He stepped into the water and the Psion hung back.

"Are you coming or not?"

Miles danced back and forth behind the Psion, waiting to see if this worked.

The Psion drifted closer to the bank and Jamie reached out. When he felt the creature in his hand, he grabbed on, backed into the river, and held him tight.

"Don't like water, do you?" Jamie said, putting the Psion inches from the flowing river. He could feel the tension in the creature.

"Release me at once, or your friend dies!" the Psion screamed, struggling to both escape from Jamie's grasp and avoid the water.

Jamie moved further out into the river.

"I said release me, now!"

"Okay," Jamie said, a smile on his face, and let his grip relax. The Psion struggled to hang onto him.

"No, no. Wait. Take me back to the bank."

"I don't think so. Looks like you could use a bath." Jamie thrust his hands toward the river and the Psion screamed in agony when a drop of water splashed up from the current against the rocks.

"Looks like the bargaining position has changed a bit, eh?"

"Where's Keladry? Bring her here at once or," he thrust him down once again, "more swimming lessons."

The Psion kept looking at the bank, judging his chances. Not quite ready to surrender.

Jamie took two more steps into the now waist high water, dangling the Psion over the river.

"Okay, okay, it is done," the Psion said.

"What's done?" Jamie asked.

"Jamie," a familiar voice called, "here, I'm over here."

Jamie turned and saw Keladry standing on the far bank. Miles danced around her feet, having found some secret mouse way across. When Jamie stepped toward her, the Psion screamed.

"Take me back to the other side first. Then you can leave."

"Nope, I don't think so. Remember when you said I had no choice but to trust you? Looks like you are in the same predicament."

Fighting the current, Jamie pushed on toward Keladry. Just before reaching the bank, he came to a rock sticking out of the water. An idea popped into his head. Dropping the Psion on the rock, he pushed on toward Keladry.

"Wait, you can't leave me here," the Psion said.

Jamie laughed. "Mr. T would be so proud if he heard me say this. 'Can't' implies ability, while 'shouldn't' implies doing the right thing. Maybe you mean shouldn't? I most certainly *can* leave you. Whether I *should* or not is debatable. I'm going with leaving you, chump."

Pulling himself up onto the bank, Keladry hugged him.

"Hey, hey," Jamie said, struggling to pull away. "We hardly know each other."

"That was brilliant, Jamie," Keladry said, reaching for another hug.

"Yeah, yeah," Jamie said. "I just hope leaving him wasn't a mistake. Maybe I should've just tossed him in."

"No, Jamie," Keladry shook her head. "We are not like them. Remember that. Now let's get out of here."

"Hey, what about me?" Miles said. "You gonna just leave me behind with the likes of them?"

Jamie looked at the tiny mouse. Reaching down he picked him up and put him carefully into his pocket. Miles poked his head out.

"If Duncan can have a pet dragon," Jamie said. "I can have a magical pet mouse. Come on, let's go."

Chapter 20   Return to the World

"A book?" Keladry said. "Imprisoned in a book. How imaginative."

"Ah, what is this, a mutual magic admiration society?" Jamie asked. "Shouldn't you be waving a wand, doing a dance, or mumbling some hocus pocus words and *getting Kathy out of there?*"

Keladry and Templar exchanged glances.

"My, my," Templar said. "One successful mission behind enemy lines and we have a Hercules in our presence."

"Sorry, Mr. T," Jamie said. "I just want to get Kathy back and be done with this."

Templar tilted his head.

"Okay, yeah I know, long way to go," Jamie said, catching on." How about done for today? Almost dying at the hands of these creatures is exhausting."

"Jamie's right," Duncan said, turning to Keladry. "How do we get her back?"

"Unfortunately, "Keladry said, "there is no easy way. Not that I can't do it, but I need to use caution. These are diabolical creatures with no consideration for others. They'll have built traps into her imprisonment. Once false move and, well, let's just say I need to be careful."

"Okay, so be careful, "Jamie said. "Tell me what to do."

"It would seem Mr. Jamieson has developed a taste for adrenaline," Templar said.

"I see that," Keladry said. She put her hands on Jamie's shoulders. "I know you're anxious for your friend, but I must do this my way. What I need you to do is be patient."

"But…"

"Jamie," Duncan said. "Leave it to Keladry, okay?"

Jamie sighed. "Okay, okay. I will go see what Seherin is up to. I bet she's in the middle of this."

Once Jamie was out of sight, Keladry turned to Duncan. "Do you trust me, Duncan?"

"Of course I do," Duncan answered.

Keladry stayed silent for a moment. "Okay then, put the book on the ground and back away."

Duncan glanced at Templar, who shrugged, then looked back at Keladry.

"Trust me on this, Duncan."

Duncan paused momentarily, then rolled forward, placing the book on the ground. He looked again at Keladry, then backed away to wait next to Templar.

Keladry motioned for the two of them to move farther back.

Retrieving her wand, she closed her eyes.

Duncan and Templar stood in silence, uncertain of what would happen next.

Keladry let out a yell and then pointed her wand. A flame shot out, turning the book to ash.

"No!" Duncan yelled, wheeling through the billowing smoke. "What have you done?"

"Exactly what they didn't expect her to do," Kathy said, emerging from the smoke.

"You're okay!" Duncan yelled, almost running over Kathy with his chair as he tried to hug her.

"But the fire?" Duncan said. "What was that?"

"Like I said," Kathy smiled. "Exactly what they didn't expect. They thought you'd try magic, which would have destroyed me with the book. By using something unmagical like fire to destroy the book, Keladry broke through the magic. Sometimes, magic loses."

"My heart is still racing," Duncan said.

"So is mine," Templar added. "You might have warned us."

"I couldn't. They would have known what I was about to do. It had to be a surprise."

"How did they take you, Kathy?" Keladry asked. "Who took you?"

"I'm not sure, but I was warned they were coming for me. I knew if I tried to resist, they'd find the nest. I couldn't let that happen.

"I take it Jamie survived his ordeal."

"He did," Duncan said, "although his success made him believe he's invincible."

"Of course," Kathy said.

"Kathy, who warned you?" Templar asked.

"A hippogriff."

"A hippogriff?" Duncan said. "I met one the other day. Said she was an ally."

"Wait," Templar said, "you didn't think you should mention this to me?"

"Sorry, Mr. T, slipped my mind."

"Yeah, well, from now on, no secrets about meeting anyone. Hear me?"

Duncan nodded.

"We better get back before Jamie tries to imprison Seherin," Templar said.

"Seherin?" Keladry said. "Who is Seherin?"

"The new history teacher, "Templar said. "Gryphon Seherin…Oh my, how did I miss that?"

"Miss what?" Duncan asked.

Keladry looked at Kathy and Duncan. "You both met a hippogriff?"

They both nodded.

"Well then, you do have an ally in this hippogriff," Keladry said. "And a very powerful one."

"We do?" Duncan said.

"Yes, Duncan," Keladry nodded. Hippogriffs are formidable allies, and…" she paused momentarily, "Gryphon is another name for Hippogriff."

"Really?" Duncan said. "In that case, we'd better go find Jamie before he makes a fool of himself. I want to thank Ms. Seherin."

"No! Duncan," Keladry said, "you cannot let her know you know. She must reveal herself to you. Hippogriffs are powerful but temperamental. She chooses to help you but will leave if anyone uncovers her identity. Especially the non-magical."

"So, we can't tell Jamie?" Duncan said.

"Exactly," Keladry nodded.

"Hmm, that may pose a problem."

"One of many, my boy," Templar said. "And not the most pressing. Time to get back. We have bigger things to tackle besides an overprotective and misguided, but sincere, teenager."

As the group started toward the school, a pair of eyes shone in the woods. Then another, and then several more.

With the group out of earshot, a figure emerged from the woods. Tall, lanky, more skeleton than human, with a raspy dark voice.

"So, a hippogriff sides with the dragons," the voice said. "How interesting...and useful." The creature motioned for the others to show themselves.

"We know the nest is around here. Cloaked, of course. One of you will remain nearby to keep watch. When they return, wait until they reveal the location, then appear to them as a hippogriff. Do not do anything other than confirm the nest's location. Let's use this unexpected hippogriff-dragon cooperation to our advantage."

One of the creatures spun in circles, transforming into a hippogriff.

"Excellent, " the voice said. "Now conceal yourself and wait. The rest of you, come with me."

As the creatures started down the path, they morphed into a group of students.

"We will hide in plain sight," the voice said, looking like a fifteen-year-old. "And we will choose the time and place to capture the dragon seeker and his dragon."

Chapter 21   Refocusing on the Goal

"Are you sure?" Jamie said, looking back at Ms. Seherin as she left the school. "I think I should follow her."

"No, ignore her," Duncan said. "I'm gonna need help with Destiny."

"Oh, no. I'm not playing fetch again," Jamie said, backing away.

"Nothing like that," Duncan said, then a smile crossed his face. "Well, maybe just once more."

"Forget it, not happening." Jamie folded his arms and turned away just in time to see Destiny bending over him. He moved just in time to avoid the drool.

"Okay, no games," Duncan said. "Let's go, I need you to help me with something."

"This doesn't involve me with dragon eggs, does it?"

"Nope, you and I have to come up with names for the new dragons," Duncan said, rolling into the school study hall.

"Why here?" Jamie asked. "What is this place?"

Duncan stared at Jamie. "Because it's a good spot to…wait a minute. Are you telling me you've never come to study hall?"

Jamie shrugged. "Never had to, I absorb everything right up here," tapping his temple.

"Oh, yeah. As reflected in your stellar academic record," Duncan said, pulling out his laptop.

"Exactly. So, we name them, eh? How about Jamie for the first one?"

"Maybe," Duncan said, opening a Google search screen, "But we need to learn about dragon history first. Seems to me there has to be some method to how they are named."

"What's the big deal?" Jamie said, flopping into a chair. "We name them Jamie, Duncan, and Merrill for the boys and Kathy, Keladry, and ah, I don't know, how about Margaret, like your mom, for the girls?"

Duncan pulled his laptop close to his chest, looking at Jamie. "I forgot to mention something important."

"Oh yeah? What's that?" Jamie said, trying to balance himself on the back legs of the chair.

"Kathy told me it could be a hundred eggs."

"What the…" Jamie said, losing his balance and tumbling backward, drawing the attention of the now annoyed study hall monitor.

"Mr. Haworth," she said, "as pleased, not to mention shocked, as I am to see you in study hall, we have rules. Pick the chair up, sit in it like a normal human, and stop disturbing others or you'll be asked to leave, which would be a new record for the shortest career in study hall since education began."

"Sorry," Jamie said, trying to ignore the giggles of the others. Putting the chair back on all four legs, he sat back down, leaning over to Duncan.

"Did you say a hundred? How the heck are we gonna come up with a hundred names?"

Duncan typed away on the keyboard. "That's what I'm trying to find out…"

"Hmm," Jamie said, "I might have an idea…"

Chapter 22   History Doesn't Repeat, it Rhymes

Duncan, Kathy, and Jamie waited near the feeding shed as Destiny devoured an enormous meal.

"I hope the food holds out," Duncan said. "There's not much left and I don't know where Mr. T went."

"He'll be back soon," Kathy said. "He and Keladry had something to do. But I'm sure they won't be gone long. It's almost time."

"Time?" Duncan said. "How do you know?"

"Because she's eating more," Kathy said, dumping more feed into the plastic kid's pool turned feeding bowl. "They do that when they are close to nesting time."

"But I'm not ready," Duncan said. "I've no idea what to do."

"No worries, we will help you."

"We, what'd ya mean we?" Jamie said, backing away. "I am no kid-wife."

"Mid-wife," Duncan said.

"Whatever," Jamie said. "I ain't that either," walking away.

Kathy pointed a finger and Jamie froze, unable to move. "Take your pick, help Duncan and I or right after Destiny finishes dinner we play fetch the dummy again. And it may not be so gentle this time."

"Okay, okay," Jamie said, hands up in surrender.

"There's a good boy," Kathy said, releasing the hold. "Now Duncan have you thought of the naming process?"

Duncan nodded. "You may find this hard to believe, but it was Jamie's idea how to do it."

Kathy glanced at Jamie, who bowed.

"Please, enlighten me on this most unexpected development."

"Jamie, would you like the honors?" Duncan asked.

"Of course, and I shall keep the explanation simple so even you can understand it, Kathy."

Kathy smiled. "Destiny, fetch time!"

"Whoa, whoa, just kidding," Jamie said, head snapping between Kathy and Destiny.

"Okay, here's what we learned. Dragons trace their lineage by the direction of their birth. In other words, as the egg comes out it will orient itself to one of the main compass points, north, south, east, and west.

"Since we have no way of knowing how many eggs will come out, we divide them into the direction they select. Once all the eggs are out we can use the dragon language, something Duncan speaks but not me, which has forty-two letters to assign a letter along with the direction.

"For example, North ah, give me the first couple of letters, Duncan."

"Alagra, Brach, Centa" Duncan said.

"Okay, so the first north egg would be Alagra North, then Brach North, then Centa North. Now, I may not be the smartest kid in the class, but I do know numbers. Four directions times forty-two letters equals one hundred sixty eight names. Each direction would have forty-two names."

"And if more arrive?" Kathy asked.

"We simply add another name starting at the other end of the alphabet. Duncan, what's the last letter?"

"Ah, ZZegra."

"So north dragon forty- three would be Alagra ZZegra North. Through the magic of math, we'd have an unlimited number of names. Forty-two times forty-two equals one thousand seven hundred sixty-four names for each direction using two letters."

"I am impressed," Kathy said.

"I do have one question," Jamie said.

"What's that?" Kathy asked.

"How are we gonna remember which egg is which?"

Kathy smiled. "Therein lies the magic of dragons. With each egg all we have to do is whisper their name to them and they will remember. It will be imprinted in the mind and recognizable by all other dragons."

"Wow," Jamie said, "an instant contact list."

"Where did you come up with this shockingly unexpected moment of genius?" Kathy asked.

"That was Duncan's doing."

Kathy looked at Duncan, who shrugged. "When we were looking into the history of dragons, we found the information about how they orient in certain directions. I said something about compounding numbers. Jamie took it from there."

"Well, Mr. T will be pleased and impressed," Kathy said. "Now let's get over to the nest and work on the delivery process. Destiny looks like she's gonna nap, which may mean it's getting even closer to her time. We better get a move on."

As they made their way down the path, Duncan turned to see Destiny flat on her back, little puffs of smoke rising from her lips, matching her breathing, then she faded into invisibility.

*****

Kathy glanced around and was ready to unveil the nest when Duncan grabbed her hand.

"What is it?" she asked.

"I don't know. I can sense something is watching us. Don't summon the nest." Then a voice came to him. Remember what I said about not all creatures being what they appear to be. Ask its name and the truth will be revealed.

"Duncan," Kathy said, "Duncan! What is it?"

"A warning from a friend, I think."

"What kind of warning?" Jamie asked.

"We may be about to find out," Kathy said, tilting her head toward the woods at the sound of breaking branches.

Duncan pulled Kathy closer and whispered. "Can you fake it?"

"Fake what?" Kathy said, pulling away.

"Fake summoning the nest, Create a false one?"

"A false one, ah, yeah. I can do that. Why?"

"Trust me on this, okay," Duncan said.

Kathy nodded.

And with a wave of her wand a doppelganger nest appeared a short distance from where the real nest remained hidden.

Duncan waited, studying the tree line for movement. Shaking leaves and bending branches caught his eye.

The hippogriff slowly came into view, wings extended, head high, and approached them. Bending one knee, the creature bowed his head.

"Greetings, Dragon Seeker. I bring you great news of our allegiance."

"And what is this news?" Duncan asked.

"The hippogriffs put ourselves at your service. Ask of us anything and it shall be done."

Duncan recalled the words of Seherin in hippogriff form. 'While I will be here to help you, I can do no more than offer my advice.'

"And your name? What shall I call you?" Duncan said.

The creature hesitated, fighting an urge, then blurted out, "I am called Lugo Ubilaz by my kind."

Kathy bent down to whisper in her ear. "Ah, Duncan…"

"I know," he answered, "I know."

"Know what?" Jamie said. "Is somebody gonna clue me in here."

Kathy moved closer to Jamie, whispering. "This creature is not a friend."

"Okay, thanks for that." Jamie took on his most imposing look.

Kathy almost laughed. "How about you let Duncan and I handle this. If we need you, we'll let you know."

Duncan rolled away from the creature and toward the fake nest. Placing his hand on the twisted mass of sticks and mud, he looked at the creature.

"Can you stand guard here?" Duncan asked. "Protect this nest from all who would do it harm while we ready the inside?"

Duncan detected the slightest smile opening on the creature's face, then fading away.

"As you say, so I shall do," Lugo said and began patrolling the perimeter of the nest.

"Can you put us inside, Kathy," Duncan winked. "We have much to do." Then he motioned for Jamie to come over.

"Go find Mr. T and fill him in. Kathy and I will keep him busy. I want to see what happens."

"I think I should stay here," tilting his head toward the creature. "He doesn't scare me."

"No, I need you to tell Mr. T," Duncan said. "Did you hear the creature's name?"

"Yeah, Luigi something. Or loogie. He's a big loogie."

"No, no. It's Lugo. Lugo Ubilaz. Tell Mr. T that. Can you remember?"

"Yeah, I got it," Jamie said.

"Okay then, go!" Duncan said pushing him toward the path. "And hurry. I've a feeling we won't be alone with this one for long."

Jamie glanced at the patrolling hippogriff, then ran off down the path. Duncan saw the creature watching Jamie, then resumed his patrol.

Floating up inside the nest, Kathy and Duncan made a show of moving sticks and creating the sounds of frenzied activity.

"So, what do you think?" Kathy asked.

"Well, if Keladry is right about Seherin being an ally, when I met her in hippogriff form she told me she could only offer advice. I think it was her voice I heard when I sensed something in the woods.

"This one is taking actions. I think it is a trap to find the nest. And I fear they'll be others here soon enough. They left this one behind to keep watch and they somehow knew about my contact with a hippogriff."

"Maybe factions exist within the hippogriffs as among the dragons," Kathy said.

"Maybe. Or maybe these are entirely different creatures. We need to be cautious." Duncan peered over the edge enough to see the tops of the creature's wings in motion.

"I think he's waiting for others to return before he does anything. For now, he's convinced he's tricked us."

"What do you want to do?" Kathy asked.

"Can you whisk us out of here and make it sound like someone's still working in the nest?" Duncan asked.

"Of course I can."

"Okay," Duncan glanced again. "How about you get us into the woods where we can see but not be seen. Let them make the first move."

"No sooner said than done," Kathy said, waving her hand.

Chapter 23   A Friend Within and Without

Jamie ran into the principal's office, out of breath and wheezing from exertion.

"My, my," Mr. T's secretary said. "Gym classes must be much harder than when I was in school. Sit, Mr. Haworth, sit down and rest."

"No…time…can't…need…to…see…Mr. T."

"I really think you should…"

"Send the boy in, Magia," Mr. T said, "it's fine."

Jamie smiled and walked into the inner sanctum.

"What have you done now?" Mr. T asked. "Whose wrath are you fleeing."

"Nothing like that," Jamie said, catching his breath. He glanced back at the door then moved closer to the desk.

"Trouble back at the nest. A hippogriff is there with Duncan and Kathy. They think it is a trick to find the nest. Kathy made up a false one to stall them while I came and got you. Come on, we need to get back," and headed toward the door.

Mr. T waved his hand, and the door closed before Jamie could get to it.

"Tell me everything, Jamie. If we go rushing in blindly, it won't help anyone. What did Duncan send you here to tell me?"

"Oh yeah," Jamie said, collapsing in a chair. "He wanted me to tell you the creature's name. It was Lugo. Lugo Umb…Lugo…"

Mr. T rose from his chair and came around. He put his hand on Jamie's shoulder. "Is it Lugo Ubilaz?"

"Yeah! That's it. Do you know him?" Jamie said, now breathing almost normally.

"I know of him and his kind. Lugo Ubilaz means 'hidden evil' in the old language. One of the weaknesses of these creatures is they cannot lie about their name. If they are asked, they must answer truthfully. Duncan must have somehow figured it out. Both he and Kathy would recognize it, but the creature may not know this."

"So, what do we do?" Jamie said. "We can't just leave them with Umberto Lipschitz."

"Lugo Ubilaz," Templar said.

"Whatever, we can't not do anything."

"Of course not, Mr. Haworth. But we need to use caution. These are powerful, devious creatures. What we need is a diversion."

"A what?" Jamie asked.

Mr. T rolled his eyes. "Something to draw the creature away long enough for Kathy to move the real nest to another location."

"How about I get the creature to chase me? You know, run up, punch him in the snout, and run."

"Mr. Haworth, your courage is admirable, but your level of in-depth planning is lacking. How are you going to outrun a creature with the body and speed of a lion that can fly? No, this requires stealth and cunning."

"Sorry, Mr. T. I'm worried for my friends."

"Of course you are, Jamie. We'll need help with this. Wait here for a moment." Mr. T left the office and spoke to his secretary. She dashed out of the office faster than Jamie ever imagined she could.

Several moments later, the secretary returned, sipping a cup of tea as if nothing had happened.

Then, a creature strode into the outer office. Templar's secretary, oblivious to this mythical creature passing by her desk, packed her bag, put on her coat, and left as if this were just another late afternoon at the high school.

Jamie looked at Templar, furrowing his brow. "Wha? What the hell is that?"

"A hippogriff, my boy. Isn't she magnificent?"

"Not the word I would choose," Jamie said, slinking behind Mr. T.

"No worries. She's been with me for years. If you ever see her surprised or frightened, run."

"And you keep her here?" Jamie asked.

"I don't keep her anywhere. Such creatures cannot be kept. One has to earn their trust."

The hippogriff came into Templar's inner office.

Jamie slid further into the shadows of the room.

"Calm down, Mr. Haworth. We have no taste for humans," and a smile crossed her face, "yet."

"That's enough of that, Gryphon," Templar said, "Jamie has demonstrated his worth in our endeavor, thus my willingness to unveil your existence to him.

"But we need to deal with this problem. One of your kind, or more likely a creature pretending to be one of you, was spying near the nest location.

"Duncan apparently sensed a trap, and they managed to delay a confrontation. But if this creature is merely a watcher, others will come."

"I can assure you, Myrrdin, no hippogriff would act in such a matter. While we've had our differences with the dragon, deception is not our way of things." She turned to Jamie.

"Come here, Jamie."

Jamie pulled back further.

"I already said I won't eat you," the Hippogriff said. "Since Myrrdin here seems to believe you worthy, I have a task for you."

"Trust her, Jamie," Templar said. "Would someone who uses my old name, known only to true friends, be anything else but an ally?"

Jamie came out of the shadow and approached the hippogriff. Towering over him, Jamie had to lean back to look into her eyes.

"I am going to put myself in your care, Mr. Haworth," the hippogriff said. "I will be vulnerable and need protection. Can you do that?"

Jamie looked at the fierce creature before him. "You want *me* to protect *you?*"

The hippogriff nodded. "That is exactly what I am asking. Will you take me to the nest area?"

Jamie glanced at Templar then back at the creature. "Ah, how am I going to do that?"

Out of the corner of his eye, Jamie saw Templar step back. Then a thundering noise shattered the quiet, and a cloud of smoke enveloped the room.

Jamie looked around, but the hippogriff was gone. Then, another sound broke through. Smoke alarms began ringing everywhere.

"Where'd she go?" Jamie asked.

"Down here, Mr. Haworth," a voice reached him from a tiny, child's toy-sized hippogriff on the floor.

"Pick her up, Jamie," Templar said. " Gently, please. Put her in your pocket and get going. I'll be along shortly, once I explain again to the fire department about an errant science experiment."

Jamie bent down, letting the miniature creature climb into his hands. "Are you sure about this, Mr. T?"

"I am, now go. And be careful."

"Okay, okay, I got it," Jamie said, running out the door. As he made it to the exit, a crowd of unfamiliar students blocked his way.

"Move, move, I gotta go," Jamie said, pushing his way through.

"You're not goin' anywhere," one said.

"Step aside, young man," Templar said, standing at the entrance to his office. "Now!"

The group parted in the middle, allowing Jamie to pass. Once Jamie was out of sight, Templar turned back to the group of students.

They had disappeared.

Oh my, we've lost the element of surprise, Templar thought. Time for more reinforcements.

Chapter 24   The Best Defense

"Those weren't students," the hippogriff said, her voice muffled but distinct.

"No kidding," Jamie said. "What do you think they were?"

"No doubt a problem for us. Stay in the woods when you get close to the nest area. If I know Myrrdin, he's figured this out as well and will bring more help."

As Jamie made his way through the woods, he kept looking over his shoulder.

"See something?" the hippogriff asked, her tiny head protruding from Jamie's shirt pocket.

"No, but I can feel something."

"Are you sure you're not magical?"

"I'd like to think I am, but my history would say otherwise."

"I think you might surprise yourself someday, Jamie. I see great potential."

As he came closer to the clearing, he knelt down to peer over a fallen tree.

"See anything?"

"The hippogriff, or whatever it is, is marching around the nest. I don't see Duncan or Kathy."

"These creatures are not very bright. It wouldn't have taken much for them to fool him into believing the nest is real.

"My guess is they're nearby. Probably doing the same as us, waiting for the others to arrive."

"Okay, now what?" Jamie asked.

"We wait."

It seemed like hours, but it was just a few minutes. The same group of students they'd met at the school came walking down the path.

The hippogriff walked over to greet them.

"The others are in the nest," he said. "No one else has shown up."

The leader of the group now morphed into a less appealing form. Tall, lanky, covered with a flowing robe over its body and bearing a protruding head without a neck, the creature stood looking up into the nest.

He turned his back on the nest and beckoned for unseen figures to come from the woods.

Two more creatures emerged, dragging Myrrdin Templar, then tossing him to the ground. Templar struggled to rise but couldn't.

With a wave of the creature's hand, the nest shattered, raining debris everywhere.

"You can show yourselves now, Dragon Seeker. Or watch your mentor here suffer an inglorious and yet unimaginably painful death. Your choice. Your pathetic attempt to fool us failed."

Jamie rose.

"Wait, Jamie," the hippogriff said, now returned to full size. "Look at Templar. Look hard."

"I've got to get out there," Jamie said, struggling to move past Seherin.

"Look, Jamie, look!"

Jamie leaned around the enormous hippogriff to look at Templar. It took a moment, but then he saw it.

"It's not him," Jamie said. "It's not Templar."

"Indeed, it is not, Mr. Haworth," the real Templar said, now kneeling behind him. "These are creatures of deception not power. Their strength lies in fooling their opponent not overpowering them."

"So, if they have no power, let's just go take them on," Jamie said.

"I didn't say they had no power," Templar said. "I told you their power is in deception. It can be just as powerful, if not more so, than anything else.

"If I know Duncan, he'll call their bluff. What we can't do is let them trick anyone into revealing the real nest. Just sit and wait. I've always wanted to watch myself die."

"What?" Jamie said.

"Metaphorically speaking, of course," Templar said. "This could be quite enlightening."

Turning his attention back to the creatures, Templar could sense their frustration. It only took a moment for the leader to lose his patience. Moving toward the prostrate and appropriately terrified fake Templar, the leader sent a jolt through the apparition which screamed quite convincingly.

"I don't sound like that, do I?" Templar said.

Jamie giggled. "You do, Mr. T, you do."

"Oh my, this is embarrassing."

After more threats, and listening to some pitiful pleadings for mercy, it was clear the ruse failed. Forcing their hand, the creatures made a production of dispatching the prisoner.

"This is on you, Dragon Seeker," it screamed before administering the faux coup de grâce.

"My, my that was entertaining, wasn't it?" Templar said.

"In a very weird way, Mr. T," Jamie said. "In a very weird way. But now what?"

"Now, we use our superior position to confront these creatures. They are not the brains behind this, but they will know who it is. Ready, Gryphon?"

"Gryphon? Who is Gryphon," Jamie asked.

"I am," the hippogriff answered. "I thought you'd never ask."

Chapter 25   The Fury of Righteousness

"What is she gonna do?" Jamie asked. "Shouldn't we go with her?"

"Just watch, my boy," Templar said. "And you'd be wise to keep this in mind when your insatiable appetite for mayhem overcomes your minimal common sense."

"Huh?" Jamie said.

Mr. Templar spun him around. "Just watch and learn what a hippogriff can do."

Gryphon came out from behind the bushes, rising to her full height. With one mighty flap of her wings, she flew into the midst of these startled creatures.

"Who are you?" one creature said, while the others circled the new arrival. "You have no business here, hippogriff."

"I do when someone like you impersonates one of my kind. We make it a policy not to interfere in other's affairs, but when something affects our standing in the world. We act with ferocity."

Without taking her eyes off the leader, she still sensed where each of the other creatures stood. Lashing out with her rear paw, one of the creatures crumbled to the ground. The others pulled back, trying to avoid a similar fate.

Spinning on her heels, she leaped into the air, knocking two more creatures senseless and sending the others fleeing.

All that remained was the leader. He tried to run but failed. Gryphon was on him in a flash, pinning him to the ground.

"Struggle all you like; your magic is powerless over me. You'll survive," Gryphon said, a grin appearing on her face, "If you answer our questions."

"Our questions?" the creature said. "I see no other…"

"Not so tough now, are ya pal?" Jamie said, standing over the prostrate creature.

Soon, Templar, Duncan, and Kathy joined the circle.

Tightening her clawed grip on the creature's neck, Gryphon said, "I will ask you this once, and you will answer me without hesitation," tightening the grip again, "or you'll be looking for a new head. Understand?"

The creature nodded, struggling to breathe.

"Who sent you?" Seherin asked, relaxing her hold.

"I, I, don't know who…"

Before the creature could finish, the hippogriff squeezed harder.

"Wait, wait," came the muffled and choking plea.

"Let it speak," Duncan said. "It's no good to us dead."

The hippogriff relaxed her grip once again, then lifted the creature into the air. "Who sent you? Answer me, or the next thing you feel will be falling from several thousand feet in the air."

Okay, okay," the creature said, massaging and trying to clear his throat. "I don't know the names," he said, holding up his hands as he felt the grip tighten." But I know what they are, and where."

The hippogriff placed him back on the ground. "Go on."

"In the deep woods along the river where the dam sits just below the bridge, there is a secret entrance into a cave. You'll find them inside."

"We'll find who?" Duncan asked.

"The Manticore and the Raven Queen," the creature answered.

And at that moment, they all knew things were about to get worse for everybody.

The hippogriff looked at the others. "You know these other beings?"

"Sadly," Duncan said. "But first, what do we do with him? We can't let him warn them."

"I want no part of this anymore," the creature pleaded. "I will gather the others and return to our own time."

"I like her idea of dropping the creep from ten thousand feet," Jamie said. "We can watch him splatter."

"How colorful an image, Mr. Jamieson," Templar said. "But that would make us no better than them. We can come up with something more creative and less homicidal?"

Jami smiled. "Technically, since they are not human, it wouldn't be homicide. I'd say cruelty to animals at worse."

"Oh, wonderful," Templar said. "Now he's a lawyer. Remember what The Bard said, First, let's kill all the lawyers."

"Who?" Jamie asked.

"Never mind, never mind," Templar said, trying to ignore him.

An idea occurred to Duncan, and he whispered to Templar. "Excellent idea, my boy. Let me know when you're ready."

Duncan approached the creature. "Summon the others back here. No tricks, or you will all fly without wings."

The creature called with a sound like a wounded animal, and the others appeared from the woods.

"Stand together," Duncan said, pointing a spot away from the shed.

Gathering into a tight group, the creatures awaited their fate.

"Hit it, Mr. T," Duncan said.

Templar waved his hand, and a cloud of smoke engulfed the creatures. When the smoke cleared, they were all gone.

"What did you do with them?" Jamie asked. "Vaporize them? Cool!"

"Nothing quite so barbarically science fiction, Jamie," Templar said. "Sorry to disappoint. Duncan thought since they were from a different time, we couldn't risk they might return here again. So…"

"So, you did vaporize them!"

"No!" Templar said. "I did send them back in time. Just not to their time. If my aim was good, they are with a friend of yours, Jamie, as we speak."

"A friend of mine?" Jamie said, confused.

Templar smiled. "Yes, they are now introducing themselves to the Psion on a very crowded rock in a river somewhere in the past. I do hope they enjoy each other's company."

"Wow, now that is cool," Jamie said. "Almost better than vaporizing them."

"I'm so glad you approve," Templar said. "Now onto more serious matters. How do we deal with our old friends?"

The group remained silent, with Jamie glancing at each of them. "Would *now* be a good time to vaporize them?"

Templar shook his head.

"First," Duncan said, "we need to move the nest just in case one of those creatures finds their way back. Then, we find a way to deal with the Manticore and Raven."

Chapter 26   Old Friends and Enemies

"Are you sure it's safe here?" Duncan asked.

"Hidden in plain sight," Kathy said, admiring her work of placing the nest on top of the shed where they kept Destiny's food. "Convenient and concealed."

"I hope you're right," Duncan said. "Now that we know Core and Harper have returned, they'll have all sorts of allies to use against us."

"Forewarned is forearmed as they say," Kathy said. "Let's get to class. Hopefully Mr. T has come up with a plan to deal with them."

Kathy turned back to face the nest. Destiny, her head resting on the edge, gave a weak smile then fell asleep.

"Hmm," Kathy said.

"What?" Duncan asked.

"I think her time is coming even sooner than I thought. My guess is we have only a day or so and she will start laying her eggs. We are going to be very busy for the next few days."

"How am I going to explain being away for days to my parents? They don't like me to be away for an hour without checking on me.

"My mother wanted me to wear a locator tag. My dad talked her out of it, but I always suspected it was all an act, and he hid one in my chair."

"Duncan" Kathy said, hands on her hips, "don't you think if your parents had put a locator on your chair, they might have noticed you flying all over the place on a dragon and said something? You know, like hey Duncan, how'd you get your chair up to 40,000 feet flying at 200 miles per hour? Stop being so paranoid."

"Yeah, you're right."

"Besides," Kathy said, a sly smile crossing her face. "They'd just enable location tracking on your phone."

Duncan stopped dead.

"Kidding, I'm just kidding. Come on, there's Mr. T," pointing toward the school.

The two made their way to the school entrance.

"Ah, here you two are," Mr. T said. "I was just filling in our new friend the hippogriff here on our two friends the Manticore and Raven Queen, also known as Harper and Core."

"Out here? Where *everybody* can see you?" Duncan said, glancing around.

"Everyone can see *us*," Mr. T said. "She here is more selective."

"Ah," Duncan said. "So, what are we gonna do about Core and Harper?

"They do sound challenging," the hippogriff said.

"Challenging?" Duncan said. "If by challenging you mean they tried to kill me and steal the egg, then yeah, they are challenging.

"Core, I'm sure Mr. T told you, was the principal here and he and Harper, a teacher who turned out to be the

Raven Queen, kidnapped Jamie and did all sorts of things to get the egg. Challenging is a bit of an understatement."

The hippogriff studied the boy, taking his measure. *He is unusual,* she thought, *not the least bit intimidated by her or anything else. I can see why he was chosen.*

"Remember, young dragon seeker, I will be nearby should a need arise." And she disappeared in a cloud of smoke.

Templar waved the smoke away. "Thank goodness we met outside, two accidental fire alarms in one day and the fire department would not be thrilled with me."

"What's next, Mr. T?" Kathy asked. "How do we deal with Core and Harper?"

"Forewarned is forearmed, I always say."

"Jeez, you guys mimicking each other all the time is frightening," Duncan said.

"Brilliant minds," Kathy added.

"Okay, first you two head off to class then…" Mr. T stopped mid-sentence and looked at Duncan. "What are you looking at?"

Duncan turned away from the building, reaching for his phone. "Don't look but second floor last window at the corner, someone is watching us."

Kathy and Templar looked.

"Hey, I said *don't* look. Don't as in do not." He typed away on the keyboard.

"Can you put the phone down for a moment and tell us what you saw?" Templar said.

"Hold on, I'm texting Jamie. He's in study hall, or he's supposed to be, I asked him to sneak down the hall and look in the room."

"Is that wise?" Templar asked, "Given his penchant for overreacting to everything."

Duncan shrugged. "We'll soon find out."

Five minutes later, Duncan's phone beeped. "Nothing, he saw nothing but..."

"But what?" Kathy said, leaning over Duncan's shoulder. Her face blanched.

"What is it?" Templar said.

"Jamie said the room was empty but when he walked in," Kathy said, "but it felt like a refrigerator, and we all know the air conditioning here isn't exactly state of the art."

Templar looked at Kathy. "You think...?"

"What else could it be?" she answered.

"Is someone gonna let the guy everybody wants to kidnap or kill know what's going on?" Duncan said.

Chapter 27   It Is About to Get Serious

Duncan followed Templar and Kathy into his office. Between their silence and shared sullen look, Duncan started to worry.

"Come here, Duncan," Templar said, leaning against his desk.

Duncan glanced at Kathy, then rolled forward. "You're scaring me, Mr. T. What's going on?"

Templar took a deep breath, looking up at the ceiling. Duncan thought he could see a tear in his eye.

Kathy came over and put her hand on Duncan's shoulder. He saw the dread on her face.

"What I am about to tell you," Templar said, clearing his throat, "is something I had hoped never to have to do. Nobody likes to admit their failures, and this was my worst. But you have a right to know what you're facing and everything that goes along with it."

"Come on, Mr. T, how much worse can it get? I've been kidnapped, had spells put on me, and now the two whatever they are who want me dead are back. Whatever it is, we'll deal with it."

Templar glanced at Kathy, then focused back on Duncan.

"Many years ago, we believed we'd found the dragon seeker. A young woman, remarkable, intelligent, and determined like yourself.

"She began her quest for the egg much like you. Disbelieving at first, then slowly coming to embrace her destiny. She was…" the words caught in his throat as he wiped away a tear.

"She was my sister," Kathy interrupted, taking over the story. "It seemed to make sense to us that the dragon seeker would be a magical creature. We never expected a human would be selected for the task. But then, we never understood how dangerous the task would become. It wasn't until you came along that we realized the wisdom of picking someone like yourself. Those opposed to the return of the dragon would never suspect a human, let alone a young man like yourself.

"We were wrong when we assumed it was Kristin."

"Wait," Duncan said, "you have a sister?"

"Had a sister," Kathy said. "When the others learned she was the Dragon Seeker, they took her," a tear dropped from her eye. "I never saw her again."

"She's dead?" Duncan said softly, trying to fight his own tears.

"We assumed she must be," Kathy said, regaining her composure. "They had no reason to keep her alive."

"I'm sorry, Kathy," Duncan said, putting his hand over hers.

"Thank you, it was a long time ago and I've learned to live with it."

"But why are you telling me this?" Duncan asked, looking between the two.

"Because when I discovered Kristin was gone from her room, it was bitterly cold inside. But It was the middle of the summer."

"And Jamie said…"

"Yup, whatever or whoever took Kristin is here," Kathy said.

"The problem is," Templar said, "we have no idea what we're facing so we have no way of protecting you."

"How am I supposed to deal with that?" Duncan said. "It's one thing to deal with things we know, it's a whole different matter to deal with the unknown."

Templar glanced at Kathy and Duncan caught the look.

"You're not telling me everything. Come on, Mr. T, this is my life we're talking about."

"I do not like to engage in rumors or legends," Templar said. "But under the circumstances I suppose this is more than just a myth.

"Long before we thought Kristin was the dragon seeker, some suggested various others were the chosen one. All turned out to be false."

"So, they weren't me," Duncan said. "What does this have to do with anything?"

"Because all of those who were thought to be dragon seekers disappeared under strange circumstances," Templar said. "And were ever seen again. Because of this, we became very reluctant to jump to conclusions about anyone being, well, you."

"Kristin wasn't the only one?" Duncan said.

Templar shook his head. "The disappearances share one common element."

"Cold?" Duncan said.

Templar nodded.

"The legends and rumors followed," Kathy said. "Legends of a creature or a force from somewhere in the highest mountains watching for signs of the return of the dragon A hidden land where all who helped the dragon would be imprisoned."

"I never put much stock in these stories," Templar said. "I attributed them to a combination of imagination and fear, but it would seem I may have been wrong."

"So why haven't I vanished? It's not like I pose much of a challenge. I'm not magical like Kristin and I'm not exactly famous for my athletic ability."

Kathy looked at Templar. "He does have the right to know."

Templar nodded.

"Duncan," Kathy said, kneeling to meet his eyes, "we think the other disappearances were just to sow fear and terror among those of us who want to help restore the dragon. In an odd way, they were telling us we had it wrong.

"It would seem even this creature knew the real dragon seeker would appear someday. Their intentions have changed. They are far more dangerous.

"It's no longer enough to get rid of you. They want to destroy you and the *LAST* Dragon to end the return of the dragon race."

Duncan sat quietly, taking it all in. Every moment of every day since he'd learned he was the Dragon Seeker he'd had to face new challenges. This, he knew, was just another, albeit deadlier, one. Yet he knew he had no choice.

"Okay then," Duncan said. "Now that we've gotten that out, any other things you've kept from me?"

Templar and Kathy both shook their heads.

"Well then, as you two are fond of saying, forewarned is forearmed. Now we know what we're facing, who this thing is doesn't really matter, does it?"

"No," Templar said," I suppose it doesn't. You are a remarkable young man, Duncan. No one could doubt you are the Dragon Seeker. Let's gather our forces, meager as they may be, and prepare to meet our shared destiny."

"You always sound like an English Lit teacher giving a lecture, Mr. T," Duncan joked. "How about we just whoop their butts?"

Templar couldn't help but smile.

Chapter 28   Hiding from the Unknown

"So, what do we do, Mr. T?" Jamie said. "We can't let them get to Duncan."

"Thanks for stating the obvious, Mr. Haworth," Templar said, "but the issue isn't what we do but how we ensure Mr. Emeris survives to aid Destiny. Let me think a bit."

Jamie and Duncan moved to another part of the room, then motioned for Kathy to join them. Glancing back at Templar, they could see he was lost in thought.

"Do you think they know where the nest is?" Duncan asked.

Kathy shrugged. "Dunno, they were watching us to find out. If they knew where it was, they would have already tried to destroy it. But," she hesitated for a moment, "I think they want to destroy you and the nest all at the same time."

Duncan just stared at her.

"They went after Kristin because we never got to this stage. I think they knew she wasn't the true Dragon Seeker. They likely know Destiny is close, and you'll stay nearby. You're the key to their success."

"So, we feed them some bogus info," Jamie said. "A disinformation campaign."

"And how do we do that?" Duncan said.

"Easy, get up," Jamie answered, pulling Duncan's arm.

Duncan shrugged him off. "Not time for your warped sense of humor, Jamie. This is serious."

Kathy smiled. "He's right Duncan. You're gonna get out of the chair in a manner of speaking."

"And what, crawl to the nest?"

"Nope," Kathy said. "Jamie here, by some miracle, has come up with the perfect solution. Do you still have that OHRV your father altered for you?"

"Yeah," Duncan answered. "Why?"

"And is it still in your garage?"

"Yeah," Duncan said, drawing out the answer.

"So, this is what we'll do," Kathy said. "Tomorrow morning, early, you and I will go for a ride. I'll use magic to get us flying again. Meanwhile, Jamie here will sneak into the woods near the river.

"I think I can maneuver around enough to make it hard for them to follow us. I'll stay low, in the tree cover. I'll let them stay close, but not too close. Make them think we're heading to the nest.

"Then, we'll land, you and Jamie will trade places, with a little help from my magic, and while they are following us you will get to the real nest. Sounds good?"

"Jamie's gonna be me?" Duncan said, "he doesn't look anything like me."

"That's true, you're a dork and I'm handsome," Jamie said.

Kathy rolled her eyes. "Not to worry. You'll both wear the same baseball hat. I'll be flying around so fast they won't get a good look until it's too late."

"But then I'll be alone with Destiny. What happens if she starts laying eggs?

"Look, Duncan, I will find a way to get back as soon as I can and help. The worst case is you must handle the first few by yourself. You can do it."

Chapter 29   The Best Laid Plans Part II

"Ready, Jamie?" Kathy asked, standing next to the OHRV.

Jamie nodded, helping Duncan out of the OHRV and into his chair.

"You sure this is gonna work?" Duncan said, his head on a swivel, looking back and forth, trying to see through the trees.

"No, but we have no other options."

"Something occurred to me last night," Duncan said. "It is a bit of a problem."

"What's that?" Kathy asked.

"While you and Jamie are flying around in the OHRV, and my wheelchair is in the back seat, how am I supposed to get to the nest? It might take a while to crawl. Like a week or so."

Kathy smiled. "Jamie thought of that as well. Jamie, show him."

Jamie reached into his pocket and out came Miles the Magical Mouse. "Your steed has arrived."

"Steed?" Duncan said, "It's a mouse. How am I gonna ride a mouse? And where did he come from?"

"Miles saved me when I went back for Keladry. I couldn't leave him, and I figured if you could have a dragon, I could have a magical mouse."

Duncan chuckled. "You are a unique one, Jamie. So, how do we do this?"

"Miles," Jamie said, placing him on the ground, "ready?"

"Always," Miles said.

Kathy moved her hand over Duncan and Miles. A bright flash of light followed.

Duncan found himself in a saddle of sorts on the mouse's back. Towering over him, Jamie now sat in his place in the OHRV, wheelchair safely onboard the OHRV.

"What the…?"

"If I were you, I'd get going," Jamie said, leaning down to get closer. "And look out for cats, hawks, and owls. Oh, and snakes, they're the sneaky ones. Don't want you two ending up as a snack."

"Thanks a lot, Jamie. Kathy, you sure about this?" Duncan said, hanging on tightly to the saddle as Miles danced around.

"I'm sure Jamie's right about you'd better get going. I just learned this miniaturization spell from Keladry and don't know how long it lasts. You need to be in the nest when it wears off. It won't be good for staying hidden if you're still on Miles when it does."

"Not to mention it won't be good for me," Miles said. "We are outta here. I didn't leave home to end up squashed by someone I hardly know."

And with that, the miniature mounted mouse cavalry disappeared into the underbrush.

As they watched them go, Kathy felt a sudden chill.

"Did you feel that?" she asked.

"I did," Jamie answered, looking round from the seat of the OHRV where Duncan had been a moment ago. "We better go too.

Chapter 30   Now What?

"You sure she's not gonna eat me?" Miles said, hiding behind Duncan. "She looks hungry."

"Destiny?" Duncan said, still adjusting to his freedom of movement inside the nest. "Nah, she always looks that way. She has plenty of food," he paused for a moment, "unless we run out."

Miles smirked, if a mouse is capable of such a display. "Funny, very funny. You're all a bunch of comedians. How about I go up to the edge of the nest and keep a look out?"

"Good idea. I have no idea how long we have to wait. I hope Kathy gets here soon; I am not sure about what I'm doing."

At that moment, Templar's voice reached them from outside the nest. A sort of insistent loud whisper.

"Duncan!, Duncan! Are you in there?"

Duncan peered over the edge. Templar stood below, glancing repeatedly over his shoulder.

"Here, Mr. T. Come on up."

Templar glanced around once more, then floated up into the nest. When he saw Duncan freely moving about, he was startled.

"Cool, eh, Mr. T? In here I can walk, sort of."

"I can see that," Templar said. "I'm not as familiar with how things work here as Kathy or Keladry. But I' glad you're enjoying the experience." He paused, not wanting to cast a pall over the moment. "But remember why you're here and this freedom of movement cannot last forever."

"I know, Mr. T, I'll be back in my chair soon enough."

"Hey," Miles said, scampering along the edge until he was close to Templar. "If you're such a great wizard, why don't you just use magic to fix Duncan?"

"I'm afraid it is not that simple, my little friend. Duncan is not broken; it is just his destiny. There are things even magic cannot fix, at least not good magic. Some practice darker forms. But nothing is without cost. Non est liberum prandium. There is no free lunch."

"So, where's Kathy?"

"I'm afraid I have unsettling news, Duncan."

"What?" Duncan said.

Templar moved closer, putting his arm around Duncan. "Kathy and Jamie are missing. They never came back after they made the switch. Your OHRV is back in your garage, but there is no sign of either of them. I've brought your chair and hidden it nearby."

"I've got to go find them," Duncan said, heading toward the nest edge. "We have to go, Mr. T."

"I'm sorry, my boy, but you can't leave. Once the process starts the Dragon Seeker must stay with the nest. Even if I wanted to let you go after them, it is out of my hands."

"But Mr. T, there's time. Nothing's started yet. I can't leave them…" Before Duncan could finish his sentence, Destiny laid down next to him. A soft whimper escaped her lips, and she looked at him for comfort, resting her head on his lap.

"It would appear Destiny's time has come, Duncan," Templar said. "This is something you have to handle on your own. No one but a Dragon Seeker may handle the eggs when they first emerge."

Duncan cradled Destiny's head. "But I thought Kathy would be here with me."

"She would have, but she could only watch until you place the eggs in the nest. This is your destiny, Duncan. Something you and the *LAST* Dragon must share alone."

And with that, Destiny gave another whimper, and the first egg appeared ....

Chapter 31   Some Things Cannot Changed

"You sure he'll be okay?" Miles said, looking back as the nest faded from view.

"Some things we all must do alone. They cannot be changed. He is a true Dragon Seeker. He will find his way."

"Now what?" Miles asked.

"Now, we go find out what happened to Kathy and Jamie. Let's hope this is not one of those moments where history repeats itself."

*****

Duncan placed each egg on the soft down of the nest, separating them by the direction of their birth. He never felt so alone and frightened. Despite all the things he'd experienced up to this moment, despite all the wild imagined stories he'd written, he never thought he'd find himself alone with a dragon giving birth.

Birth to eggs that were his responsibility to protect.

Destiny's voice echoed in his head. "Remember, Duncan, you must select the *LAST* Dragon egg from among the first to arrive."

Now surrounded by many eggs, several for each direction of the compass, Duncan struggled to see signs of any difference. How do I decide? How do I know which one to pick? How do I choose an egg with a living dragon that may lie dormant for eons?

Facing a choice he once dreaded made it all the worse. Why me? Why me?

"Because you *are* the Dragon Seeker, Duncan Emeris," Destiny's voice rose again "You are chosen and have it within you to follow this path. I know all my children, and the one you choose as the *LAST* Dragon will be in good hands.

"Listen to your heart. See what is right before you. Those who chose you chose well."

Duncan studied the eggs. He remembered when he first saw the shiny signs of the *LAST* egg as he rode Balinor over Diamond Hill. It seemed like it was so long ago, yet it was less than a year. How the direction of his life had changed so much.

Changing direction echoed in his mind. Changing direction was a key to his dilemma. Changing directions.

"I've got it," he said out loud. Destiny raised her head and gave a weak smile. "I knew you would, Duncan,' she said, they lay back down.

Duncan waited for the next egg. He knew this was the one to be the *LAST* Dragon. As the egg emerged, unlike the four before her, the egg continued to turn not settling on one direction.

Duncan waited for a sign, something to tell him he was right about this. And then he saw it, the slight hesitation at the same point. And he knew.

Reaching for the egg, he cradled it in his arms. A soft glow emanated from within. He placed the egg in the nest facing straight up, pointing to the stars now shining overhead.

A new direction, he thought. A new direction for the dragons. A journey to a new future, not condemned to repeat the past.

He hoped he'd made the right choice. But some things are only time reveals.

Chapter 32   Calculated Risks

"I feared we would find this to be the case," Templar said, peeking into the entrance of the cave.

"Feared what?" Miles said, sitting on Templar's shoulder.

"Can you feel the cold, Miles?"

"Yeah, isn't that just the coolness of the cave?"

"Not *that* cold," Templar answered. "If our friend from the last encounter at the nest didn't lie to us, inside that cave is a Manticore, a Raven Queen, and, as I suspected, their new ally."

"Ally?"

"Yes, yes, the cold is a sign. I don't have time to explain but suffice it to say whatever causes that chill is the worst of our problems. We can't fight what we don't understand."

Miles glanced at the cave, then back at Templar. "We need to know what's inside, right?"

"Yeah, but how we find out is the problem."

Miles took a deep breath then let it out slowly. "Some things we have to do alone, right? That's what you said."

"I did," Templar answered, eyes narrowing. "Why?"

Miles scampered down and headed toward the cave. "Now must be my turn. I'll be right back, I hope." Keeping as much in the shadows as he could, Miles disappeared into the cave.

It seemed like an eternity to Templar, but Miles appeared, unscathed, a few moments later.,

"That was very brave of you, my friend," Templar said. "If a bit reckless."

"Yeah, well. Nothing ventured, nothing gained. Jeez, it is freezing in there. But I have learned something."

"Do tell."

"You are right. The Manticore and Raven Queen, along with an enormous number of actual ravens, are inside. This made me rather nervous because I wasn't sure if ravens eat mice."

"Yes," Templar nodded, "that would have been terribly inconvenient for me."

Miles closed one eye and cocked his head, looking at Templar, who shrugged.

"Anyway," Mile continued, "it's hard to describe the other creature but it appears mostly shimmering waves of light. The cold is much worse when it moves about.

"It was obvious the other two are afraid of it. They kept a distance from it. Staying near a fire for warmth. But I did notice one thing."

"What's that?" Templar asked.

"This creature avoided getting too close to the fire. Not sure if it was the heat or the light that it wanted to avoid but it stayed in shadows away from the flames."

"Hmm, that may be useful. Any signs of our friends? The fact that the Manticore and Raven Queen even have a fire going would indicate this is more an alliance of convenience. They do not trust this cold creature."

"I didn't see anyone else, but the cave is deep, and I could see light coming from the back. They may be deeper inside. I might be able to get in there, if you could find a way to draw the others away from the cave."

"Let me think about that. I'm not sure we should risk you going back inside."

"Look, Jamie saved me from a rather painful, unpleasant existence back where I came from. I owe him. You draw them out of the cave; I'll get inside and find our friends."

Templar thought for a moment, then arrived at his decision.

"Okay, my brave friend. It would appear we will face our destiny together. Give me a moment to think this through."

Templar made his way around to the top of the cave entrance. Unaccustomed to doing things without deliberation, his uncertainty almost paralyzed him.

Regaining his composure, he stood up, placed his hands together, and mouthed some words. At first nothing happened, then Miles felt the ground begin to shake. Gently at first, then building in intensity until the water was sloshing over the dam and rocks fell near the entrance.

Miles watched as the Manticore and Raven Queen emerged. They looked around for the cause of the commotion.

"Ah," the Manticore said, "if it isn't our old friend Myrddin Templar come to visit. Is this your idea of a rescue mission?"

The Raven Queen took to the sky with her army, the screeching noise grating on Miles's ears, landing in the still quivering trees surrounding the entrance.

"Perhaps," she said, "you'd like to meet our new friend, Gifrōren?"

With that, a shimmering packet of light appeared from the cave, swarming toward Templar. Before the creature could close on him, Templar produced a flame in his hands, wielding it as a shield.

The creature hesitated, hovering outside of the heat and light.

The Manticore laughed. "Do you really think you can fight all three of us? Why go through all that? Just join us. Or perhaps you'd prefer to meet the same fate as awaits your friends who are our guests…for the moment."

Miles, watching the action from the shadows, dashed into the cave, now certain the others were inside.

"Join you?" Templar said. "Never. I'm just getting started." And with that the flame grew in intensity and size as he hurled it toward Gifrōren.

Startled by the flame, the creature retreated. Templar then hurled more flame into the tree where the ravens sat, igniting it.

In the mounting confusion, before they had a chance to recover, Templar disappeared.

"Find him," the Gifrōren said. "Now!"

"Shouldn't one of us stay here?" the Manticore said.

"No need. He's alone. We know the Dragon Seeker is in the nest. He cannot help him, and we have the others."

At that, the Manticore ran off in pursuit followed by the raven flock. The Gifrōren sealed the cave entrance, then followed the others.

Templar watched from a hiding spot on the top of the cave. He knew they expected him to flee. Always give them what they expect, he thought. Reappearing, he knew the deception would only last a short time.

On his way down, he put out the fire in the tree hoping it had attracted no human attention.

Making his way to the front of the cave, he studied the seal on the entrance. Cold and solid to touch, he needed to unseal his friends inside before the others returned.

Chapter 33   One Step Behind

"Did you really think we'd fall for your pathetic attempt at deception?" The Gifrōren's voice caught Templar by surprise.

Templar spun around, raising his hand to reignite the flame, but it was too late. Ensnared as if frozen, he couldn't move.

"There's always hope," Templar said.

"Not for you anymore, Templar, not for you or your friends inside. Let's join them, shall we?"

Keeping his focus on Templar, he unsealed the cave. Just as he caught Templar by surprise, Jamie, Kathy, and Miles dashing from the cave surprised him.

Wielding a torch Jamie thrust it at the Gifrōren, driving him back.

"Can you move, Mr. T?" Jamie yelled, waving the torch back and forth.

"Sorry to say, I cannot," Templar said. "Go, run, get away, Jamie. There are more important things at stake here than me and the others."

"Yes, Jamie," the Gifrōren hissed. "Run away, enjoy your momentary freedom. I'll deal with you later."

Surprising Jamie with his speed, the Gifrōren disappeared into cave dragging Templar with him. In a flash the entrance was sealed, then it vanished.

"They're gone," Jamie said. "They're all gone! The cave is gone."

"Let's get out of here, Jamie," Kathy said. "The Manticore and Raven Queen will be back, and we can't do anything about this right now. Come on."

Jamie took one last look at where the cave had been, tossing the torch into the river. The hissing of the dying flame reminded Jamie of the Gifrōren's voice as it faded away.

Then the three were off.

Chapter 34   The Gathering Storm

"Wait here," Miles said, then ran off, leaving Jamie and Kathy watching from the woods.

Until one tries to watch a mouse in a hurry, you can't understand how hard it can be. They would glimpse gray fur or a flash of movement but other than that they had no idea where Miles was or where he was headed.

Then, for just the briefest of moments, they saw him run up to the top of the old storage shed and disappear.

"What the…?" Jamie said. "Where did he go?"

"He's in the nest," Kathy said, wondering how Miles knew about the nest.

"The nest is on the shed?"

"Yup, hidden in plain sight," Kathy answered.

"I'm back," Miles interrupted.

Jamie nearly fell over. "Holy shit, you scared me half to death. How'd you do that?"

Miles tilted his head and waited for Jamie's brain to catch up.

While this conversation went on, Kathy studied the mouse. How did he know about the nest?

"Oh yeah," Jamie finally caught on, "magical mouse. Now what?"

"Now we wait."

"Wait? I ain't waiting for nothing. We gotta do something."

"And we will, Jamie," another voice startling him.

The hippogriff now stood next to them in the woods. For such large creatures they are remarkably quiet, Jamie thought.

"Yes, we are, Jamie. Part of our ability to survive."

"You can read my mind?" Jamie said.

"I don't have to read anything," the hippogriff said. "I can hear your thoughts."

"Well, that could be awkward. Would it be too much to ask for you guys to stop sneaking up on me?" Jamie said, trying to slow his breathing.

"Perhaps you should be more mindful of your surroundings," the hippogriff answered. "But we've no time for what I fear would be a long learning curve." She turned back to face Miles. "Is the Dragon Seeker ready?"

Miles nodded.

"Okay, go tell him to come here when he is certain the egg laying is over. It will give me time to plan our next move."

Miles ran off back to the nest, while the hippogriff circled the ground a few times, folded her wings, and curled up on the ground.

"That's it? We're just gonna sit here?" Jamie said.

The hippogriff locked onto Jamie's eyes. "Young man, your courage is admirable, but it will also get you killed if you rush into things blindly.

"What chance do you stand against such magical beings? Especially this Gifrōren that has been capturing and disposing of creatures such as yourself rather horribly for millennia?

"We wait for the Dragon Seeker, and then you and he will act. I suggest you rest now. Won't be any time for it later."

"Duncan and I?" Jamie said. "Aren't you gonna help?"

"No, I can only act in defense of the hippogriff. Kathy and I will guard the eggs until the Dragon Seeker returns. If he returns."

"Shouldn't I go with them?" Kathy said. "I have skills to fight such creatures."

"Magic cannot defeat magic," the hippogriff said.

"What can then?" Kathy asked.

"Something only these two can do," the hippogriff said. "If they can see beyond their self-imposed limitations."

With that, the hippogriff closed her eyes and fell asleep.

Duncan looked at his two friends, unsure of his next move.

"What do you think?" he asked.

Jamie shrugged, putting his hand out in a gesture of uncertainty.

Kathy stayed silent for a moment. Then sat down. "Might as well do what she says, we are gonna get very busy when Duncan emerges from the nest.

*****

"Kathy? Jamie?" Duncan said, waking them from their rest, "What's happened?"

Kathy brought Duncan up to speed.

"Then what are we waiting for?" Duncan said. "let's go find Keladry and all go get Mr. T. The two of you have powerful magic."

She shook her head. "The hippogriff is right. Magic won't help. Magic has been at the heart of our problem this whole time. Much as I'd like to help. Much as I know Keladry would want to. I am uncertain what will happen. We cannot help you."

Stepping forward, she kissed Duncan on the forehead and touched Jamie on his shoulder.

"This you two must do alone, together. Come back to us, Duncan. There is so much more for you to do."

And with a wave of her hand, she floated up into the air, disappearing into the nest, followed by the hippogriff.

"Well, that was hardly fair," Jamie said.

"What?" Duncan asked.

"The ugly guy gets a kiss, and the handsome hero gets a pat on the back," Jamie said, smiling.

Duncan chuckled. "She was probably afraid of getting germs from you."

Chapter 35   Baiting the Trap

"Of course, they'll come for you," the Gifrōren said. "Those who think of themselves as good cannot help but act nobly...and die trying."

"They'll gather some compatriots, formulate a plan, stage an attack and...fail." The Gifrōren came within inches of Templar's face, the bitter cold freezing patches of skin as he struggled against the bonds.

"We will be waiting for them. They will join the others who've failed before them. And then, the Dragon Seeker and the eggs will be defenseless. We'll put an end to the dragon so it can never return."

A noise caught his attention, forcing him to turn away. "Right on time, I see. Enjoy your final moments, Templar, you haven't many left."

The Gifrōren faded into a shimmering wave of light and moved toward the cave entrance.

His voice echoed off the walls. "Hmm, should I let them find their own way in or make it easy for them? Choices, choices..."

*****

"Are you sure about this?" Jamie said. "It's a solid wall of rock. The cave is gone."

"It's not gone, Jamie," Duncan said, "it's hidden. It might look solid, but it's a trick. And if I understand the

Gifrōren, he's waiting inside for us to come to him. Mr. T is the bait for this trap."

"Bait? Trap? So why are we thinking about falling into a trap?"

"We're not gonna fall into anything," Duncan said, his eyes focused on the wall before him. "We're gonna bring him to us."

"So, what are we gonna do?" Jamie asked, glancing over at the rock wall trying to see what Duncan saw.

"What they do not expect," Duncan said. "You stay here, I'll let you know when I need you to do something," rolling around the wall into the open.

"What are you doing?" Jamie said. "They'll see us."

"They'll see me. That's what I want them to do," Duncan said. He leaned over, picked up a rock, and threw it at the rock wall.

The rock bounced off the wall, almost hitting Jamie.

"Hey, I thought you said it was a trick? Seems solid to me."

"Sorry," Duncan said, grabbing another rock. "You might want to duck," throwing the rock against the wall.

"I'm right here!" he yelled. "I'm the one you want. Come on out."

Templar strained against the magic, trying to call out but nothing happened. He could see Duncan through the cloaked entrance but could do nothing to warn him.

The Gifrōren appeared again.

"It would seem I underestimated their stupidity. I never imagined the Dragon Seeker himself would show up. The other one, yes. He's impulsive and loyal, a dangerous combination. But Emeris? How surprisingly foolish for someone selected to protect the dragon." The Gifrōren floated toward the entrance, hesitating a moment.

"Perhaps I should let him struggle a bit. He is a resourceful, if foolish, boy. Let him find his way in and we can both enjoy Emeris becoming my prisoner," the Gifrōren's face morphed into what some might take as a smile. "A brief moment as a captive before I rid the world of this would be Dragon savior."

Jamie watched Duncan heave another rock at the wall.

"Ah, Duncan," Jamie said, "you do know the definition of insanity is performing the same act over and over expecting a different result, don't you? Maybe the rock isn't working?"

Duncan smirked. "Look, he's taunting me, wants me to find a way in. If I do that we're playing on his court. He'll grow impatient if we do nothing. We'll force him to act, put some uncertainty into play." He reached down and tossed another rock.

The pile of rocks continued growing at the base of the wall, but the cave remained sealed.

"Now what?" Jamie whispered, chin resting on his hand as he watched Duncan reach for another rock.

At first, the vibrations were almost imperceptible, growing in intensity until Duncan's chair bounced as if on a trampoline.

Jamie started toward his friend, but Duncan waved him off. "Stay there, let him come to me. He's just trying to scare us off."

The rock wall began to shimmer then faded into black. The entrance to the cave now visible, the tremors slowed then stopped.

A deathly, unnatural silence enveloped them. Duncan glanced back to see Jamie moving along the edge of the ridge toward the cave entrance. He tried calling out, but no sound emerged from his mouth.

The wave of cold brought his attention back to the entrance. Bone-chilling, unnaturally piercing, Duncan shivered in his chair.

He looked into the darkness, but saw nothing, except a few leaves and twigs falling from the top of the cave. Then a flickering light, dim at first then growing in intensity appeared deep in the cave.

A voice, echoing off the walls, reached his ears.

"Alright, Mr. Emeris, I'll play your pathetic little game," the Gifrōren said. "I see you're struggling with the cold. Well, it's going to get much worse than that for you I'm afraid."

The Gifrōren now floated just inside the entrance. "Why don't you just roll on in here and save us both a lot of wasted time. A pathetic creature like you cannot hope to challenge me. You can't even walk. What are you gonna do, run me over?"

A single twig drifted down from the top of the cave and Duncan glanced up to see Jamie holding a huge bundle of sticks and twigs.

Mr. T is right, Duncan thought, Jamie is crazy but he's all I got right now.

Duncan turned his attention back to the Gifrōren.

"How about you come get me? It may not be as easy as you think."

The Gifrōren made a sound that might pass for a sigh, then emerged from the cave. As the creature started toward Duncan, an avalanche of dried leaves, twigs, and branches rained down enveloping the creature and the ground around it.

"Wanna play ball, scarecrow?" Jamie said, in a poor imitation of the Wicked Witch of the West, as he tossed a burning bundle of twigs onto the creature.

Caught by surprise, the Gifrōren moved to get away from the flames, clearing the entrance to the cave. Jamie jumped down and handed Duncan a burning stick.

"Hold him off with this, I'll get Mr. T."

"How you gonna do that?" Duncan said, waving the flame toward the Gifrōren and lighting small patches of grass on fire around him to keep the creature off balance.

"Haven't thought that far in advance," Jamie said, disappearing into the dark of the cave, his makeshift torchlight fading as he went deeper inside.

Chapter 36   A Nagging Feeling

"That was freaking cool," Jamie said, leading the way down the path. "Did you see the look on the Gifrōren's face when I rained fire on him? I terrified him."

Templer and Duncan remained silent, oblivious to their friend's recounting of the rescue.

"Hey," Jamie said, stopping just before they reached the school. "I may not be magical like you guys but give me some credit here for taking on Mr. Frosty."

"Yes, yes, you did good, Mr. Haworth," Templar said. "The problem is not you."

"Problem?" Jamie asked. "What problem?"

"Duncan," Templar said, ignoring Jamie for the moment. "What's wrong?"

Duncan twisted side to side in his chair as if looking for someone behind them. "It was too easy, Mr. T. Sure the Gifrōren seems terrified of fire, but come on. A creature that powerful lets us practically walk out of there with you?

"Something's not right."

Templar nodded. "I agree. There's something amiss here."

"Oh sure, it couldn't be I did something heroic," Jamie said. "No, of course not. That couldn't possibly be true."

"Stop with the pity party, Mr. Haworth. Your actions were heroic. Facing such a creature took courage. This is no reflection on you.

"But we have to face facts. If the Gifrōren wanted, you'd be an iceberg right now. You had no way of knowing that wouldn't happen, yet you still stood up to him."

"Thanks," Jamie smiled. "So, what's the problem?"

"The problem," Duncan said, "is the Gifrōren let us get away with it for a reason. We need to figure out why before we do anything else."

Jamie thought for a moment. "A tracker!"

"What?" Templar asked.

"Somehow, the Gifrōren is tracking us or…"

"Or what, Jamie, spit it out," Templar said.

"Or you, Mr. T. I bet he's tracking you, hoping you'll lead him to the nest."

Duncan and Templar exchanged glances.

"Just when I think you can't surprise me anymore, Mr. Haworth," Templar said, "you do."

"But how? How is he tracking you?" Jamie said.

"Duncan? This is your time to rise to the occasion, again," Templar said, moving away and spinning around. "Find it."

Duncan remained motionless for the moment, lost in thought. "When you were in the cave, did the Gifrōren take anything from you?"

Templar shook his head. "Not that I recall. But there were moments when I was in darkness unable to see or hear."

"A spell, perhaps?" Duncan said.

"Possibly, but I would be sensitive to such things. It must be something he put on me. Something so innocuous as to be overlooked."

"Maybe we're overthinking this," Jamie said. "I mean, remember what you said, Duncan, about uncertainty. Maybe it's just that. Spread a little doubt between us.

"Think about it. If we suspected he was tracking Mr. T, he'd avoid going to the nest. That's one less person who can defend the eggs. Without doing anything he is splitting our forces. Deny and conquer."

"Mr. Haworth, you never cease to amaze me," Templar said, "for a variety of reasons. It's divide and conquer, but your version works as well. The problem is how do we mitigate this doubt. If by some unknown magic he is tracking me, then I certainly can't go to the nest. And if he is not tracking me, and we have no way of knowing that to be true, I still can't go to the nest."

"Doubt wins," Jamie said.

"Not necessarily," Duncan said. "It's true, for the moment, we can't take the chance. But, as you always say, Mr. T, forewarned is forearmed.

"We can set a trap for the Gifrōren. Lure him to the nest, or what he'll think is the nest, and find a way to imprison him."

"The hard part is how we do that," Templar said. "This Gifrōren is a powerful and dangerous creature. Containing him will not be easy."

"But not impossible, either," Duncan said. "I need to return to the nest. You guys stay here. I'll explain to Kathy what's happened, and we'll come up with something."

Duncan rolled off, his head moving back and forth, scanning the surroundings. Enemies were everywhere, or so it seemed.

Doubt is an insidious force, yet determination is equal to the challenge.

Chapter 37   Everything Has a Weakness

"Duncan!" Kathy said, appearing aside the still invisible nest, "I was starting to worry. How's Mr. T?"

"Fine, now that we warmed him up. How are things here?"

"Destiny's resting. By my count there are eighty-five eggs. So, putting the *LAST* egg aside, that's eighty-four new dragons ready to come into the world. Forty-two females and forty-two males, you did well."

"I didn't do anything; Destiny had the hard part. I was just arranging them in the nest. Forty-two, huh, funny, it's the meaning of life from the Hitchhiker's Guide to the Universe. Maybe that's a sign."

"Let's hope. Why didn't Mr. T and Jamie come with you?"

Duncan looked around, making sure they were alone. Although one could never be sure.

"Yeah, well we've got another problem. Make sure your cloaking spell stays in place on the nest for the time being."

"Why, what's the problem?" Kathy asked, now doing her own surveilling of the area.

"When Jamie and I managed to get Mr. T free from the Gifrōren, we realized it was too easy. It's like he let us get away with it. We think he's either tracking Mr. T somehow or wants us to think he is. It creates a dilemma for us."

"I'd say. Smart of Mr. T to avoid coming here." Kathy motioned for Duncan to follow her. After walking down the trail and into the woods, she sat on a fallen tree.

"Best we avoid spending too much time in the open near the nest. I'm pretty sure no one saw us, but just to be safe."

"That leads us to the next problem," Duncan said, rocking his chair to get it flat on the soft piles of fallen leaves. "How do we capture this Gifrōren and get rid of him?"

"That won't be easy. I saw how terrified the Manticore and Raven Queen were of it. For those two to be afraid, he must be very powerful. But…" her look went off to the distance, brow furrowed.

"What? What are you thinking?"

"Everything has a weaknesses and limitations, right?"

"Obviously," Duncan said, arms outstretched, palms up.

Kathy smiled. "I don't see that as your weakness or limitation. But that's for another time. We know the Gifrōren shies away from fire. Yet, it isn't a complete weakness, it merely distracts him."

"Yeah," Duncan said, leaning forward in his chair.

"I don't think it's the fire itself he fears."

"You don't?"

"No, it's not the flame, it's the heat. His power is from the terrible cold within him. If the rumors of him coming from up north in the high mountains are true, it makes sense. He draws power from the cold.

"And what happens when heat and cold come in contact?"

"The cold heats up!' Duncan said.

"Well, technically the warmer surface cools down and establishes a balance between them. Come on, you know this from physics. The higher energy from the heat moves to the cooler surface increasing the kinetic energy. Entropy always increases."

"Oh yeah, that's right. You're starting to sound like Mr. T. But how does this help us? We're not in physics right now."

Kathy reached over and gave him a whack on the head.

"Ouch, hey. What was that for?" Duncan said, rubbing his head.

"Pay attention. If the Gifrōren somehow draws energy from the cold, how I have no idea, but it doesn't matter, and we heat him up, he'll grow weaker. At least that's my premise."

"And if you're wrong?" Duncan said, putting himself out of her reach.

"Plan B," she said.

"What's plan B?"

Kathy shrugged. "Haven't got one yet, still refining plan A."

"Great."

"Okay, let's go find Mr. T and Jamie. I'll get a message to the hippogriff to come guard the area while we're away.

"What about Destiny? Shouldn't one of us stay with her and the eggs?"

Kathy stood up and brushed off leaves from her jeans. "Duncan, you've seen what a dragon is capable of when angered. Can you imagine what a dragon would do if someone tried to harm their eggs? She'll be fine now that all the eggs are here. And I know for certain she won't let anyone or anything near them."

Duncan hesitated for a moment, then started to roll his chair back to the path.

He's no longer just Duncan, Kathy thought, he is the Dragon Seeker and, more than that, the Guardian of the Dragon.

Chapter 38   A Cataclysmic Decision

"Hmm," Templar said, "sounds like it might work. Then again, I taught English Literature and Creative Writing, physics was never my forte'"

"But it makes sense," Kathy said. "Why else would he keep fire around if not just to try and trick us?"

Templar nodded, stroking his neck. "So how do we immolate this creature?"

"We ain't gonna immolate 'em," Jamie said. "We're gonna fry him."

Templar started to correct Jamie, his mouth opened as he tried to come up with a simple explanation, but then reality kicked in. "Of course, we are, Jamie," he sighed, "of course we are."

"I have an idea," Jamie said, encouraged by Templar's reply.

Templar rolled his eyes. "I know I will regret this, but what is the brilliant idea of yours?"

Jamie smiled. "A flame thrower. I've seen them in old war movies. I bet I could build one."

"And likely immolate yourself in the process I'm afraid," Templar said. "Although…"

"Mr. T!" Duncan said, "Really?"

"Sorry, momentarily lapse in my moral compass." He turned to face Jamie. "How about we look for a less weapons-of-mass-destruction-like solution to this dilemma?"

"Aww," Jamie said, disappointed in his being denied his big moment.

"What we need is something less obvious than Jamie acting like Rambo," Duncan said. "A trap where the Gifrōren doesn't suspect anything."

"We know the Gifrōren wants the location of the nest," Kathy said. "Let's give it to him."

"You mean create a decoy?" Duncan said.

"No," Kathy shook her head. "The Gifrōren would see through the magic. The only reason he hasn't found the nest is because he's unable to leave the cave for long periods of time. That's why he's using the Raven Queen and Manticore. They are his eyes and ears. He needs them to find the location before he risks leaving the area of the cave.

"We use the real nest. With him away from the cave, he'll be vulnerable It's the only way."

"I don't know, Kathy," Duncan said. "We're not sure this is gonna work. What happens if it doesn't? How long do you think we can hold him off before he makes us all prisoners?

"There's gotta be another way. What do you think, Mr. T?"

"Unfortunately, Duncan, I think she's right. This Gifrōren will not stop until he has the eggs, Destiny, and you. We either face this now or we'll never be able to protect the eggs until they hatch."

Duncan sat back in his chair, looking between Templar and Kathy.

"How about Keladry? Can't she help?"

"Duncan," Templar said, patting him on the shoulder. "Keladry is still weak from her captivity, but even if she wasn't, she can't help us.

"This is again fallen to you. We will all do as much as we can, but you and Destiny are the ones who must face the Gifrōren and protect the eggs."

"I still think my flamethrower is a better idea," Jamie said, breaking the tension. "Barbecued Gifrōren anyone?"

Even Duncan had to smile, but inside all he felt was dread.

Chapter 39   A Plan, Such as it Is

"Water ballons?" Duncan asked, tilting his head. "How do water balloons help?"

"Simple," Jamie smiled. "We fill 'em with gasoline. Drop them onto the Gifrōren and spark 'em up."

"And do you think this Gifrōren is just gonna stand there while we throw these balloons at him?"

"No, of course not. We lure him near the nest. You and Destiny act like you are ready to fight him. Meanwhile, I'll hide in a tree with a bag full of these balloons. The Gifrōren floats into range, I drop the balloons, and Destiny does what dragons do best."

"I don't know, Jamie. Something's bothering me about this whole idea."

"That's just nerves. Look, we got this. Trust me."

"I trust you, Jamie. It's just I've learned to trust my instincts as well."

"Look, Kathy and Mr. T say this is the only way. I'm not letting you do this alone. We can do this, Duncan. I know we can."

"Okay, I'm going to check on Destiny. Come get me when everything is ready."

*****

"You really think this will work?" Duncan said.

Kathy shrugged, sitting among the pulsating eggs. "I think it is our best shot. I've had the hippogriff keeping an eye on the area. The Raven Queen and Manticore have been searching for us all over.

"Soon as I uncloak the nest, they'll see it and tell the Gifrōren. Once that happens, it will be all up to you and Jamie."

A short while later, Jamie voice reached out to them. "We're all set down here."

"Ready?" Kathy asked.

"As we'll ever be," Duncan said, leaning against Destiny and rubbing her neck.

"Okay, let's go." Kathy waved her hand and the three appeared outside the nest.

Jamie and Mr. T stood at the edge of the woods.

"Come over here," Jamie said, "I need to show you the setup."

After explaining how things would work, Jamie climbed up into position.

Duncan and Destiny moved to a spot facing the path, the nest behind them. Kathy and Mr. T hid behind the shed.

"Okay," Kathy called out, "Here we go." With a wave of her hand, the nest appeared. Almost immediately the sounds of ravens calling to each other flooded the area.

The Manticore appeared from the woods, soon joined by the Raven Queen. Withing moments, a chill reached Duncan followed by a feeling of dread. He pulled Destiny closer.

The Gifrōren soon appeared, remaining just inside the tree line and just out of range of the trap.

"Do you think he knows it's a trap?" Duncan whispered out of the side of his mouth.

"Of course he knows it's a trap," Kathy said. "He's just not sure what kind."

Destiny pawed at the ground. Duncan put his hand in front of her to hold her back.

The Gifrōren started forward. Jamie shifted position and readied himself. Just before the Gifrōren reached the mark, Duncan remembered.

"Jamie, noooooo....."

But it was too late. Jamie pulled the cord, and the gas filled balloons broke over the Gifrōren.

The smile on the creature's face told Duncan he was right. Duncan lunged for Destiny, missing the now moving dragon, and falling from his chair.

Destiny reared back and sent a wall of dragon fire at the Gifrōren.

The blast sent Destiny and Dustin and his chair crashing into the shed, which collapsed. The nest now on the ground, but still intact. Smoke and fire raged over the Gifrōren as it glided forward.

Seizing Destiny, the creature then moved toward the nest. Duncan tried to struggle into his chair, but his hands burned when he touched the metal frame. The heat singed his skin.

Kathy and Mr. T came running from behind the shed trying to reach Duncan but were driven off by the heat of the conflagration.

Jamie jumped from the tree, misjudging the height, spraining his ankle. Despite the pain he hobbled over to

Duncan, pulling him away from the fire. Duncan screamed for him to let him go, but Jamie held on.

The last thing they all saw was a huge flock of ravens lifting the nest into the air while the Gifrōren carried off Destiny.

The lingering odor of smoke seemed the aroma of disaster.

Chapter 40   I Should Have Known

Gathering in Templar's office, looking more like a hospital ward than school, they sat in a sullen silence.

Jamie leaned his chin on one crutch, using the other to scratch an unreachable itch in his cast. Duncan tugged at the bandages on his hands. Kathy paced the floor.

"What do we do, Mr. T?" Jamie said, breaking the silence.

"Well, first we need…"

"This is all my fault," Duncan interrupted. "I should have known."

"No, it's not, Duncan," Kathy said. "We all agreed this was the right plan. How could we know what would happen?"

"I did," Duncan said. "But I was too late to do anything."

"You did what, my boy?" Templar said.

"Just before Jamie dropped the balloons, I remembered something about heat and cold. It's all about the vibrations of the atoms. That's where the power lies.

The Gifrōren doesn't draw power from the cold or the heat. He draws it from the entropy change. But his power is limited to what's around him. A small fire isn't enough for what he wanted to do.

"He tricked us into doing exactly what he needed. We gave him the power to do what he did. Without our help he couldn't have taken Destiny and all the eggs.

"He wanted them all and we, no I, gave him the way."

"Nonsense, my boy," Templar said. "We're dealing with diabolical forces here bent on ending the dragon. Forces that have been marshaling for eons. What we need to do is formulate another plan, albeit a more precise one."

"But why?" Duncan said, "the eggs and Destiny…" the words caught in his throat, "are already gone by now."

"I don't think so," Templar said. "If he could simply destroy them, he'd have done it there and then. No, no, I'm certain Destiny and the eggs are still very much with us.

"Where is the issue for the moment."

"I may be able to help with that," said the hippogriff as she walked into the gathering.

"How?" asked Duncan.

"I was there when all this happened. Saw it in real time. I…"

Jamie hobbled over, fuming. "And you did nothing? Just stood around watching? What kind of ally are you? You're as bad as them. You're…"

The hippogriff took a quick toward Jamie, towering over the boy.

"If you'll contain your misdirected outrage for a moment, I'll explain. But if you want to act the fool, I can just go."

"Let her talk, Jamie," Duncan said.

"Thank you, Duncan," the hippogriff bowed. "Now, as I was saying, I watched the disaster unfold. And just so you understand, I've said from the beginning I can only offer advice except under rare circumstances.

"Had you asked me about your plan, I would have agreed it was worth trying. No one could anticipate what happened. This Gifrōren is a little-known creature, few have ever been able to challenge it.

"But Myrrdin is correct, Destiny and the eggs are very believe he has a much more disturbing purpose."

"And what's that?" Duncan asked.

"The enemies of the dragon now realize destroying them is wasting an opportunity. A different approach could reap great benefits. They no longer seek to destroy them they seek to enslave them.

"They've formed an alliance with the Red Dragon and plan to use Destiny and her eggs as their slaves."

"We can't let that happen!" Duncan said. "How do we find them?"

The hippogriff smiled. "I know where the Gifrōren took them, I followed them when they took the nest."

"Where?" a chorus of voices asked in unison.

"Unfortunately, a long journey from here. I've just returned from there and it's been six days since they were taken."

'Just tell me where and I'll find a way," Duncan said.

"We'll find a way," Templar said. "We're in this together."

Jamie hobbled over to the hippogriff. "I'm sorry for what I said."

The hippogriff nodded. "No worries, Jamie. We all say things we don't mean in moments of anger. Just be sure to keep your head about you. Things are going to get very interesting."

Chapter 41   Finding Destiny

"Oh no, no way!' Jamie said. "I'm going and that's final," folding his arms and leaning against the wall.

"And how will you be any help?" Kathy said. "You can barely walk."

Jamie lifted himself off the wall, grabbed the crutches in one hand, walked to the open window, and tossed them out.

"That's how! Now let's get on with how where gonna do this. We already know who is going."

"Hey!" a voice drifted up from outside. "They almost hit me."

"Oops," Jamie said, then yelled "Sorry" out the window.

"You really are a menace," Kathy said. "You know that?"

Jamie shrugged.

"Okay, let's get down to business, shall we?" Templar said. "According to our friend, the Gifrōren has taken them back in time. A quite distant time when this whole area was under a glacier."

"Really?" Jamie said, "there was a glacier here?"

Templar rubbed his chin as he looked at Jamie. "I really need to do a better job of evaluating your teachers, Mr. Jamieson. I think they may be shortchanging you."

"Nah, I'm just kidding. I knew there were glaciers here. That's why it was so cold when Washington crossed the Potomac. Is that how far back we have to go?"

"Oh my," Kathy said, putting her arm on Templar. "Let it go, Mr. T, Let it go."

"No, Jamie, a bit further than that. Like thirty thousand years."

"How are we going to do that, Mr. T?" Duncan said.

"It won't be easy. My magic is powerful, but even that has limitations. Kathy and I have discussed this and between the two of us and with whatever help Keladry can offer, we can send two people back. But…"

"Great," Jamie said, "Duncan and I will go."

"Wait, Jamie, hold on. What's the but part, Mt. T?"

"Yes, ah, well. We are certain we can get you both there. But assuming you find Destiny and the eggs, we are uncertain if we can get you all back to this time."

A silence hung over the room as the meaning of Templar's words sunk in.

"Can you get Destiny and the eggs back?" Duncan said.

Templar looked at Kathy, then back to Duncan.

"Yes, my boy, that I am certain we can do."

"Then the decision is made. I'll go alone."

"Oh no you don't," Jamie said, moving to stand next to Duncan. "They said they can send two of us and you need my help."

"No, Jamie, I won't let you…"

"I'm afraid he's right, Duncan," Kathy said. "It will take two to defeat the Gifrōren. You can't go alone."

"Why can't you come with me? You have magic."

"Because I need to be here with Mr. T and Keladry for the magic to work. If we aren't together, we may not be able to get anyone back to our time."

Duncan looked at Jamie. "You sure you want to risk this? We may never get back here."

"Look at it this way, I'll never get detention again either. Sounds like a win to me. Remember, always look on the bright side of life."

"You are a wonder, Mr. Jamieson," Templar said. 'A genuine wonder."

"Okay now that we've settled that, how do we get there and what do we do about the Gifrōren?" Jamie said.

*****

"Ready?" Templar asked, as he, Kathy, and Keladry gathered around Duncan and Jamie. Seated in Duncan's modified OHRV they looked out of place dressed in winter clothes on this warm night.

"How did you convince your parents to dig out your winter clothes, Duncan?" Kathy asked.

"I told them we were rehearsing a play about Inuits. I'm not sure they believed me, but they went along with it."

He grew silent for a moment. I just hope it's not my last conversation with them, he thought.

"Okay, ready as we'll ever be."

Templar, Kathy, and Keladry gathered into a circle, held hands, and closed their eyes. Jamie and Duncan tried to listen to the words, but they were unlike anything they'd ever heard before.

"Shouldn't something be happening?" Jamie said.

"Wait for it, Jamie. I've a feeling it is not going to be a…."

Before the words came out, the OHRV began to shake and rock. Then, it stopped. Jamie looked at Duncan, who shrugged.

They both turned to look back at the others, when a blast of frigid air hit them and they rocketed over a blindingly white frozen landscape of solid ice mountains.

"Holy…," Jamie's voice lost in the jet stream. "Hang on!" he yelled, leaning into Duncan.

"Really?" Duncan yelled back, "Hold on? That never occurred to me."

Buffeted by the winds, Duncan fought with the controls turning it toward the surface of the glacier. Bouncing like a raft in hundred-foot seas, the OHRV careened toward the ground.

Jamie reached over and helped Duncan pull back on the stick. Sliding, bouncing, almost flipping over, the OHRV skidded along toward a large boulder embedded in the ice, before coming to a sudden stop.

"Well, that was fun," Jamie said,

"Ah yeah," Duncan said, "my thoughts exactly." Leaning over the edge, Duncan reached down to touch the surface of the glacier.

"Is your chair gonna work here?" Jamie said. "I'm not sure I can carry you."

"Nor would I let you. I'd crawl first. It's solid, the problem won't be getting the chair to move. The problem will be stopping it."

"What, you don't have snow tires?" Jamie laughed at his own humor.

"No, smartass, I don't."

Jamie reached into the back of the OHRV and pulled out a duffle bag.

"What's that?" Duncan asked.

"Dunno, Kathy handed it to me just before we left."

Reaching into the bag, Jamie pulled out a set of trekking poles, a length of rope, and a pair of crampons.

"Ah, now I know why Mr. T let you come with me," Duncan said, a smile creeping across his face. "You're my anchor. Useful dead weight."

"Oh, very funny. How about we get on with what we're here to do? I hate being cold and this is ridiculous."

Duncan pushed the seat back, opened the door, and pulled his chair close. Slipping in, his weight forced the chair to slide.

"Ah, Jamie, let me apologize for my bad humor. I think you'll be more than an anchor. You'll stop me from sliding off into a crevasse."

Jamie hurried into the crampons, took a quick walk to get used to them, then tied the rope to himself and the chair.

Moving to stand in front of Duncan, he looked around.

"I won't say it," Duncan couldn't stop the grin, "but I so want to yell, Mush!"

"You do and I will untie the rope and play hockey with you and the chair."

Duncan put up his hands in mock surrender

"Okay, that's better," Jamie said. "Where to?"

Duncan looked around. Everything was pure white except for a few giant boulders frozen in the ice. It all looked the same.

"I'm not sure," Duncan said. "But the hippogriff said it would be obvious. Nothing is obvious here except it's frigid and white."

Jamie did a complete circle looking for anything different. Nothing.

"What did the hippogriff say exactly?" he asked.

"Ah, she said it will be obvious because the Gifrōren is a creature of habit."

Jamie looked around again. Habit, he thought, habit means routine and routine means without thinking just going on autopilot. What kind of habit would a Gifrōren have?

And then he saw it.

"I got it," he said, "I got it, I think."

"Got what?" Duncan said, looking out over the unending white sameness.

"The boulders, Duncan, the boulders," Jamie said. "They're not random, they're cairns. It's a trail marker."

Duncan looked again and now it was clear. It was beyond obvious and that's why he missed it.

"But why would he leave a trail? The Gifrōren doesn't seem to me to be the type that gets lost."

"The trail is not for him, it's for whoever he's working with. The Manticore and Raven Queen perhaps. And who knows who, or what, else.

"He didn't think we'd find out where he'd taken the nest or recognize the trail."

"Jamie, you are a genius."

"As I've been trying to tell everyone."

"Ready to tempt fate again?" Duncan said, sliding his chair sideways, trying to line up on the first boulder.

"Let's go, pal. We've a dragon and eggs to save." Jamie started toward the first cairn, dragging Duncan behind him.

Chapter 42   The Meaning of Life

As they made their way from boulder to boulder, the temperature seemed to drop with each step.

"We must be getting close," Jamie said. "It's getting colder."

"If it gets much colder, my wheels are gonna freeze to the ice," Duncan said, rocking the stuck chair as Jamie tugged on the rope.

Coming over a small ridge, another series of boulders loomed in the distance.

"Oh man, there's miles to go," Jamie said, head drooping from exhaustion.

"Did someone call my name?" a muffled voice said.

"What the…" Jamie looked back a Duncan. "That isn't…?"

"Indeed, it is," Miles poked his head out of Jamie's pocket. "You didn't think I let you go without me, did you?"

"Miles? How'd you get in there?"

"Mice get into places no one would ever imagine. So, where's this Gifrōren at? Let's get Destiny and the nest and get outta here. My fur isn't exactly made for this weather."

"Miles, I'm glad you're here," Jamie said.

"This might be a problem," Duncan said, "a big problem."

"How can a little mouse be a big problem?" Jamie asked.

"Because of what Mr. T said about not being sure he could get us all back. Now there's someone else."

"But he's just a mouse," Jamie said.

"Hey, I'm a special mouse," Miles said, head tilting to the side and tiny mouse arms folded in defiance.

"Of course you are, Miles," Duncan said. "But the priority are the eggs and Destiny, not us. Your help is welcome, but you may find yourself having to get used to this cold."

Miles looked between the two boys, then scampered up to Jamie's shoulder. "In for a penny, in for a pound. What do we do?

"Apparently, we walk," Jamie said, pointing to the line of boulders, "that way."

Miles snuggled into the color of Jamie's jacket. "Size has its privileges. I'll ride."

Hours passed as the troop kept trudging along. Miles, now perched as lookout on Jamie's head, was the first to see it.

"Look, look, a cave!"

"Where?" Duncan said, craning his neck to follow Miles's line of sight.

"There, straight ahead. Just past the next boulder."

Jamie and Duncan saw it at the same time.

"Looks like the fun it is about to start," Jamie said, then spun around, looking up. "Listen, what's that?"

The sound grew louder, its source unmistakable. A rhythmic pattern of woosh, woosh. A dragon approached.

"Quick," Duncan said, "get in the shadow of the boulder, there's room for us all."

A moment later, as the group huddled in the cover, a giant Red Dragon zoomed past, coming to land at the entrance of the cave.

Folding its wings, the dragon slipped into the cave and disappeared.

"Mr. T is right," Duncan said. "They don't want to destroy the dragons in the eggs. They want to enslave them."

"We ain't gonna let that happen, are we?" Jamie said.

"Not if I can help it, but we need to know what we're facing. The red dragon is bad enough. And we know the Gifrōren is in there and probably the Manticore and Raven Queen. It's the unknown I worry about.

"Anybody got any ideas on how we can find out?"

Jamie and Duncan both looked at Miles.

"Me? You want me to go in there?" Miles said. "Alright, I'll do it. Dragon or no dragon. Gifrōren or no Gifrōren. I'm goin' in there. I may not come out, but I'll do it for Destiny and the eggs.

"I just have one thing to ask?"

"What's that?" Jamie and Duncan said in unison.

"Talk me out of it," Miles said, slinking back.

Chapter 43   An Unexpected Discovery

It seemed like hours passed while Miles was in the cave. In that time, several more flocks of ravens arrived as well as other bizarre creatures.

The enemy was building their forces; the odds were mounting against them.

"There he is," Jamie said, spotting a small brown blur running from the cave.

Miles ran up Jamie's leg and sat on his shoulders.

"Well?"

"Good news, bad news. What do you want first?"

"Go with the good news," Duncan said, "we could use some."

"Destiny and the eggs are in there."

"That's the good news?" Jamie said. "We kinda knew that."

"And…" Miles paused for effect, "there's someone else in there. A girl and there's something familiar about her."

"What?" Duncan asked. "She looks like Kathy."

At the words, Duncan took a quick breath. "It's Kristin, I know it is. Kathy's sister."

"Kathy has a sister?" Jamie said. "Why didn't you say so, we can double date."

"She's been missing for years. The Gifrōren stole her away a long time ago. We have to bring her out as well."

"Hmm," Jamie said. "we're already one over with Miles. Add her in and it looks like none of us are leaving."

"If that's the price for freeing Destiny and the eggs, then that's what will do," Duncan said. "Okay, Miles, what's the bad news?"

"There's a rather large red dragon and he seems intent on harming Destiny," Miles said. "I heard them arguing about her. The dragon said they didn't need her, and the others say they do. The Gifrōren finally stood between Destiny and the dragon to keep him at bay."

"How are we gonna get everybody out of there and back?" Duncan said. "If Mr. T and the others aren't sure they can do it, how can we?"

A long silence descended, each of them lost in the reality of their circumstances.

"We find another way," Jamie said, breaking the silence.

"You have an idea?" Duncan said.

"I have the concept of an idea."

"That's like saying you have plans for a house. You can't live in plans."

"True. But give me time. I'll come up with something."

Jamie wandered away, occasionally glancing at the cave entrance. Duncan and Miles kept watch.

"How about this…" Jamie said.

Chapter 44   A Greater Purpose

"I don't know, Jamie," Duncan said, "sounds a crazy."

"Crazy is my specialty," Jamie said, pointing his finger at his head. "And we all know how effective doubt can be. Look, if it works, the problem of getting back is solved *and* we get them back on our turf. Homecourt advantage and all."

"And if it doesn't work?" Duncan said.

"Like I said before, no more detention."

"I don't know about this. It's too risky."

"If you have a better idea," Jamie said, "I'll listen. But you're the one who made it clear getting Destiny and the eggs back is the priority. This gives us the best chance."

"Miles," Jamie said, "what do you think?"

"Well, I don't want to lose you, I'm just getting used to this whole new partnership of ours, but I think you're right. If you can pull it off, it just might work. What's detention anyway?"

Jamie chuckled. "Another specialty of mine. Okay. It's settled. Operation Traitor starts now."

Miles ran down Jamie's jacket and slid into the pocket.

"Stay quiet in there, Miles," Jamie said. "Wait until I give you the signal. Ready, Duncan?"

Duncan shrugged. "As we'll ever be. I hope you're right about this."

"Of course I'm right. What is the reason for this fight against the dragon? Greed. Pure greed. That's what motivates them and that's how we defeat them. Making them doubt their chance of success."

Duncan sat up straight in his chair and held up his right hand. Jamie gave him a high-five, then headed toward the cave.

"Jamie!" Duncan called after him. "If you don't come back, I will sell your bike!"

Jamie gave him a thumbs up, then turned toward the cave.

Here goes nothing, he thought.
*****

"What's this?" the Gifrōren hissed. "A wannabe hero come to save the day?'

Jamie fought against the terror in the pit of his stomach. Forcing himself to show no fear to the creature.

"I'm here because those wizards didn't want me to learn the truth…or share it."

"Truth? What truth?" the Gifrōren said, as the others surrounded Jamie.

"Just get rid of him," the Manticore said, "he can't be trusted."

"Let me deal with him," the Red Dragon said. "I'll enjoy watching dragonfire consume him."

"Not until I listen to his lies," the Gifrōren said. "Then I'll decide."

"Go ahead, human, tell me your woeful tale."

"Listen," Jamie said, summoning the courage to face them. "Do you think I'd just walk in here if I had another choice? They banished me because of what they didn't want me to find out. They assumed you'd finish me off and their conscience would be clear.

"But it was too late, I already knew about the other eggs they've hidden away."

"Eggs? What other eggs?" The Raven Queen said. "We know there were eighty-five eggs, and we have them all." She faced the Gifrōren. "He's lying, this is a trick. Let me finish him off."

"It would seem I have a choice to make," the Gifrōren said. "Listen to what you have to offer or pick which one of my compatriots gets to dispose of you.

"Wanna guess which way I am leaning?"

Jamie summoned all his nerve, stepping toward the Gifrōren. "Then do it. I am freaking freezing here. You'd be doing me a favor. But know this, there are more eggs. I know where they'll keep them and how to get in there, and I'd prefer to be back home. I owe them no loyalty for the way they treated me.

"Bring me back and I'll show you. And if it turns out I'm lying, you can do whatever you want. I can't stop you."

The Gifrōren studied Jamie for a long moment, floating back and forth, lost in thought.

"Okay, foolish boy, I'll indulge this for a little bit." He turned to the others. "If there are other eggs we can't succeed unless we have them all. You three go ahead of us and locate Templar and the others. I'll bring our newest guest along shortly."

"Shouldn't we leave someone here with the eggs?" the Manticore said.

"No need, we'll seal the cave when we leave. And they wouldn't dare to use magic from outside the cave, they can't risk damaging the eggs. Now go, we've wasted enough time standing around. If there are more eggs, I want them here."

Jamie watched as the others left the cave. He still hadn't seen signs of the nest or Destiny, but he knew they were somewhere inside.

"Now for you, Jamie," the Gifrōren hissed his name. "Of course, I know your name. I know all about you and this poor attempt at deception."

Jamie shrugged. "Whatever, there's nothing I can do about it. You can believe me or not, it's out of my hands."

The resignation in Jamie's voice surprised the Gifrōren. He expected begging and pleading, not surrender. The Gifrōren found humans with the capacity for self-sacrifice unlikely. Maybe there was something to this story.

With the Gifrōren's attention focused elsewhere, Jamie opened the pocket flap of his jacket and Miles scampered down into the shadows.

Just before he disappeared, Miles winked at Jamie and Jamie knew he'd heard the whole conversation. Odd the success of this plan hinged on a mouse.

Chapter 45   Without and Within

Duncan watched as the Manticore, Red Dragon, and the Raven Queen and her army leave the cave. But no Gifrōren or Jamie.

Somethings wrong, Duncan thought, the Gifrōren must have seen through the story. Now alone, he wondered what to do next.

Caught between a determination to do something and indecision as to what, Duncan sat in his chair trying to think. Just as he was ready to move into the open, something in the cave caught his eye.

Jamie, followed by the Gifrōren, emerged from the cave and backed away from the entrance. As the Gifrōren turned to face the cave, Mr. T's words about magic not being perfect popped into Duncan's head.

Duncan wondered, what if? Reaching for the trekking poles, Duncan moved as close as he dared to the entrance, keeping the boulder between him and the Gifrōren.

Jamie saw the tracks on the ice and moved to draw the Gifrōren's attention.

"Where do you think you're going?" the Gifrōren said.

"Where could I go?" Jamie answered. "It's not like I can outrun you."

The imitation of a smile crossed the Gifrōren's face. "True, very true. Now to seal things here and head back.

You are just moments away from a deciding event in your life.

"And depending on how that goes, these may be your last moments."

The Gifrōren raised its hand, then slowly lowered it. Duncan saw the cave entrance starting to fade. Indecision paralyzed him, then he forced himself to act.

Sliding the trekking pole to the mouth of the cave, he hoped that little imperfection in the Gifrōren's magic might be enough.

When Jamie caught the motion of the pole, he called out. "Hey, what happens if I am telling the truth? You'll let me go, right?"

It was enough to divert the Gifrōren's attention for a split second.

"That remains to be seen," the Gifrōren said. "But as you surmised, there is nothing you can do about it."

"Oh yeah, thanks for that."

"What did you expect?" the Gifrōren said. "We all act according to our nature. Did you think your offer of information, made from a sense of desperation not cooperation, would alter my nature?

"If the circumstances were different, do you think I'd expect you to treat *me* differently after all I've done? Of course not. Stop being foolish. You have a chance, a very small chance, but a chance to walk away from this. Don't delude yourself otherwise. What happens from here on in is up to me, you'll just have to see how that plays out."

A moment later, Duncan watched his best friend and the Gifrōren disappear.

Now he was outside a sealed cave, thousands of years in the past, in a frozen wasteland, and he was alone. Well, that wasn't true. There was the mouse.

"Hey, Duncan, you there?" Miles's voice permeated the wall, bringing him back to reality.

"Miles? Is that you?"

"Ah, who'd you expect?" Miles answered.

"Good point. I'm not sure this helped, but when the Gifrōren went to seal the cave, I slid one of the trekking poles under it. Can you see it?"

Silence.

"Miles?" Duncan said.

Silence.

"Oh, I saw it," Miles said, standing on the arm of Duncan's chair, amused by the shock on Duncan's face.

"Jeez, you scared me half to death," Duncan said. "How'd you get out here?"

"Your trick with the pole worked. There's a gap in the seal. A bit snug for the others, but hopefully a temporary obstacle."

"You found them?"

"Ah, we've already established this, Duncan. Try to keep up. Kristin, Destiny, and the eggs are inside. We are outside. I can go inside and outside. You and they cannot. With me so far?"

"Yeah, yeah. So, how do we get them out?"

"I was hoping you had an idea."

Duncan's silence offered little hope.

"I wonder…" Miles paused a minute.

"What?" Duncan asked.

"Let me go back inside. I have an idea." Miles ran down the chair, disappearing into the trekking pole tunnel."

A few moments later, a muffled voice called out. Duncan couldn't quite make out the words.

"What?' he yelled. "I can't hear what you said."

The explosion knocked Duncan out of his chair, bouncing him off the boulder. When he regained his senses, Destiny was licking his face.

"What happened," he said, struggling back into his chair.

"I warned you to back up!' Miles said.

"I couldn't hear what you said," rubbing both ears. "Now I think I'm deaf."

"Oops, sorry. It'll pass. Anyway, as I suspected there was magic hidden in the trekking poles. I'm sure Kathy did it. I don't think Mr. T would have risked it. But it worked. Pretty well from what I can see."

"Yeah, thanks for that," Duncan said, brushing dirt and rock fragments off himself.

"I take it you're Duncan," a voice said. "I'm Kristin. Thanks for getting me out of there."

"You're welcome. How's the nest?"

"Fine, I invoked a cloaking spell. Makes it easier to move."

"You still have magic?" Duncan said.

"Out here I do," Kristin said. "Inside no."

"Then how did you get the magic in the pole to work?"

"Easy, part of the pole was outside. I could get to that," Kristin said. "Now what?"

"Now we send a message back to Mr. T, Kathy, and Keladry and hope they can get us out of here."

"Kathy's there?" Kristin said.

"She is," Duncan said, "and she is gonna be thrilled to see you."

Kristin smiled. "It's been a long time."

"Okay, here it goes," Duncan reached into the hidden compartment of his chair and took out a small amulet. Holding it in his hands, he focused his thoughts on a time and place far, far away.

Chapter 46   Sacrifice

"He what?" Templar said, a look of rage on his face. "Why?"

"Because we saw no other way," Duncan said. "You told us the eggs and Destiny were the priority. The sort of implies we were expendable."

"That's not what I meant at all," Templar said.

"Well then, you should have been a wee bit clearer about that," Duncan said.

Templar ground his right fist into his left hand. "Arrrrgggh, you and Jamie will be the death of me. Where are Destiny and the eggs now?"

"I tried to think of another place the Gifrōren wouldn't know about. I took them to Keladry's place, Dungeely Close. None of us have been near there since last year.

"Where is Kathy, by the way, we have a surprise for her?"

"I think we've had enough of your surprises for one day," Templar said.

"We found Kristin,"

Templar's eyes grew wide. "She's alive?"

"Very much so," Duncan said. "She's with Destiny, Miles, and the eggs."

"Oh my, Duncan," Templar wiped tear from his eye. "One moment I want to throttle you and the next to hug you."

"How about we find Kathy and just go see Kristin," Duncan said. "I'm not the hugging type."

"Find me for what?" Kathy said, appearing as if on cue.

Templar winked at Kathy. "Come with us, Kathy. We've… I mean Duncan has something to show you."

Kathy glanced between the two. "What is it?"

"You'll see," Templar said. "Let's use conventional means of travel, though. Magic always seems to attract the wrong crowd."

Piling into Templar's ancient Volkswagen van, the three bounced along the road, soon arriving at Dungeely Close.

"Why here?" Kathy asked. "Keladry hasn't come here in months. The place is empty"

"Go look inside," Duncan said, "you too, Mr. T. I'll give you a minute."

"What is this?" Kathy said. "We've no time for one of you and Jamie's gags."

"Yes," Mr. T said, climbing out of the van. "ah, we'll tell you about Jamie in a moment. Come on with me."

Kathy looked at Duncan, then followed Templar inside.

Duncan waited a few moments, then rolled down the ramp. Making his way along the alley, he rolled up to the door, bounced himself over the stone threshold, and glided into the room.

Kathy, Kristin, and Templar were entangled in a group hug, tears flowing. Destiny hovered around the eggs, dashing back and forth, not understanding why her friends were crying.

"Oh, Duncan," Kathy said, running to hug him. "How can I ever thank you?"

"Yes, my boy," Templar said, "you've done a commendable thing," coming over to join the hug, Kristin soon in the midst too.

"Okay, okay," Duncan said, "you're crushing the guy in the wheelchair. You're welcome. Now let's figure out how to find Jamie."

"Jamie?" Kathy said, "yeah, where is Jamie? I want to thank him too."

When the story was over, Duncan was struck by Kathy's silence, and the terrifying look on her face.

After a few moments, she walked over to pet Destiny.

"Duncan," she said, without facing him. "Where did Jamie tell the Gifrōren we had hidden other eggs?"

"I don't know," Duncan said. "This was all sort of made up as we went along. I tried to talk him out of it, but you know Jamie. Once he made up his mind there was no stopping him."

Kathy spun around. "So, where would he take them? It would be somewhere hard to get to and somewhere we would know about."

Duncan shrugged.

"Myrrdin?"

"I'm at a loss as well," Templar said. "Mr. Jamieson is full of secrets. I'm not certain where he'd lead them."

Duncan remained silent for a moment while Kristin, Kathy, and Templar talked. Worried about his friend, Duncan tried to think like Jamie, it hurt his brain, but he kept at it.

With each passing moment, Duncan's dread for Jamie grew. His fingers played out a continuous rhythm on the arm of his chair.

And then it hit him. Jamie, more than anything else, was a less than enthusiastic student. He spent more time in detention in his freshman year than some kids did in four years of high school.

He'd know if he tried to lead them somewhere he wasn't intimately familiar with they'd sense it. It made sense he would take them someplace where he knew all the nooks and crannies and little-known escape routes, those he so often used to avoid being seen cutting classes.

"He's taking them to the school," Duncan said, breaking his silence.

"School?" Kathy said, "Why on earth would he…"

"Of course it's the school!" Templar interrupted. "You've got it right, Duncan. It's the last place anyone would either look for Jamie or think we'd use to hide eggs."

"But if it is the school," Kristin said, "aren't we too late? He's probably already there."

"No, he'll drag it out, hoping we figure it out," Templar said. "Invent some story about traps and alarms he has to bypass, slowing down their progress."

"Let's go!" Duncan said, heading toward the door.

"Wait, Duncan," Kathy said, "we need to think this out. If we rush in blindly, Jamie won't stand a chance. You said the Gifrōren sent the others ahead, right? To look for us?"

"Yeah," Duncan nodded.

"And they're looking for Mr. T and me?"

"Yup."

"And they never saw you there with Jamie, so they think you're with us?"

"True."

"I think it's safe to assume they don't know you freed Kristin and Destiny," Kathy said. "We can use that to spring a real trap."

"How to we do that?" Duncan said. "Every time we try something it blows up on us."

"We give them something to find," Kathy said. "We lead them to the hiding place."

"What hiding place?" Duncan said, face scrunched up in confusion.

"The one with," Kathy waved her hand back and forth and a bunch of dragon eggs appeared. "These."

"Brilliant, Kathy," Templar said. "We confirm Jamie's concocted story in their minds."

"Exactly. And then to create real chaos. We let them see Kristin. They'll panic. My guess is the Gifrōren will return to the past to check on the nest. We split their forces. Divide and conquer."

"But why would the Gifrōren leave?" Duncan said. "Why not send one of the others?"

"Because I don't think the Gifrōren can survive here very long. It would explain why there's been so little contact over the years. He is a powerful creature, but everything has limitations."

"And what happens if he takes Jamie with them?" Duncan asked. "We got lucky last time we went back there. But luck isn't something I prefer to count on."

"Here's what I think," Kathy said. "The Gifrōren's partnership with the others is a tenuous one. I think, given the opportunity, he'd just destroy the others and keep the dragons for himself. I think he needs the dragons as much as they do, but he has no choice but to work with them. They know something about him, his weaknesses or vulnerabilities, and he can't risk it."

"Any ideas what that is?" Templar said.

"Not a clue," Kathy said. "But we need to figure it out."

"Okay," Templar said, "first things first. Let's bait the trap." He piled a few eggs onto Duncan's lap and gathered as many as he could carry. The others followed. After loading them in the van, they headed off to the school.

Chapter 47   Divining the Past

As they pulled up in front of the school, Templar turned in his seat. "Kristin, stay here out of sight. We want to bring you in at the most opportune moment. Put them completely off balance.

"Kathy, would you conjure up a couple of big bags so we can hide the decoy eggs inside. I want them to guess what we're doing.

"Duncan, you head inside and check things out. If they're already here, I believe you've developed the skills to detect their presence. If they're not in there, then it gives us time.

"Ready?"

"Ready," they all said in unison.
*****

"Hmm, what's this?" the Manticore said, pointing to the school entrance.

The Raven Queen hovered just overhead. "Bringing in supplies I would guess. Maybe Jamie isn't a fraud after all. Looks like their planning on staying for a bit." She motioned with her head, and two ravens flew to her side.

"Go to the Gifrōren. Tell him the others are at the school." The ravens flew off.

Moment later, the Gifrōren arrived with Jamie in tow.

"They're here?" he hissed. "All of them?"

The Raven Queen nodded.

The Gifrōren turned to Jamie. "Where are they hidden, boy, precisely?"

Jamie took a deep breath. "I'm not sure, Templar said he would handle that. I just know they're in there."

The Gifrōren slid closer, chilling Jamie to the bone. "You know him, and you know the building. Where are they?"

Jamie struggled to think, his brain numbed by the cold. "Ah, they're, they're in the boiler room," he said, teeth chattering. "But they'll be traps near them."

The Gifrōren made a sound that could pass for a laugh. "Well, my friend, let's hope you can find these traps because it will be you suffering the effects if you set one off."

*****

"Why here, Mr. T?" Duncan said, as they placed the eggs on a makeshift nest near the giant furnace.

"This is one of Mr. Jamieson's, and a generations of students before him, favorite hiding places."

"Really? If you knew about this, why didn't you stop them from getting in here?"

"Choices. As long as I knew where they were, and they weren't creating too much of a problem and, more importantly, weren't falling behind academically, I figure it was a safer choice to let them believe they were getting away with it."

Duncan chuckled. "I may have to give up that secret, Mr. T. Too good not to torture Jamie with it."

"Let's hope you have that chance, Duncan," stealing away the humor of the moment.

"How long do we wait?" Duncan said. "It seems like a waste of time, and we can never go back. At least not without cost."

"That's it," Kathy said, "Time is the answer."

"Ah, doesn't an answer require a question?" Duncan said. "I didn't ask one."

"But you did ask a question," Kathy said. "And if I'm right, it is the perfect way to solve our problem."

Duncan looked at Templar, who shrugged.

"I'm as lost as you are, my boy. But I'm sure Kathy will enlighten us momentarily," he leaned against his desk. "Won't you, my dear?"

Kathy was lost in thought, staring out the window. Then, she turned to face them.

"Okay, here's what I'm thinking. What do we know about the Gifrōren?"

"Well, we..." Duncan started to speak but Kathy interrupted.

"We know he has two clear abilities. He can travel between two places in time, here and where he comes from, and he controls people through the cold, right?"

"Yeah, it seems..." Duncan tried again and was cut off.

"I think there's a limit to his ability to stay here. He needs to go back periodically. Like recharging a battery. He draws no power from anything here. We were wrong to think otherwise. All of it comes from the past. Being here drains his power. His pretend fear of fire is an actual smoke screen."

"And it is this vulnerability we can use to defeat him."

Duncan waited a moment. "Can I speak now?"

Kathy nodded.

"Thanks," Duncan said. "Is that why Jamie's plan backfired, no pun intended."

Templar gave an approving nod and grin.

"Yup," Kathy said.

"So, we have to find a way to what, stop him from returning here?"

"Nope, we stop him from getting back there. We need to wear him down until Keladry and I can put a containment spell on him so he can never return to gain more power.

"Then, we send him to a place he'll never be able to leave, like back to Miles's old haunt."

"I don't know, Kathy," Duncan said. "We seem to come up with what sounds like a good idea, and then it turns out not so well,"

"Trust me on this, Duncan," Kathy said, going to one knee to look into his eyes. "This all makes sense now, and I know how we do it."

"How?" Duncan and Templar both said.

"Do you know what wears him down the most?"

Duncan and Templar both leaned forward.

"Prisoners."

"Prisoners?" Duncan said. "You mean we let him take us prisoner?" he looked at Templar. "And you thought my plan was crazy."

"Let's hear her out, my boy," Templar said.

"If I am right, and I am sure I am, he seizes whoever he sees supporting the dragon. While we assumed he killed them, it would appear he does not. Perhaps he is limited in some way. It's not empathy or compassion, that's for sure.

"He took Kristin because he thought she was the Dragon Seeker. But that was wrong. He acted based on what *we* were doing. He reacts to our behavior.

"It would explain his allying himself with the Manticore and Raven Queen." Pausing a moment to gather her thoughts.

"And we know they have no compunction against harming others."

"I'm still not seeing how this helps us," Duncan said. "He may not kill things, but he still has power to control them."

"I think I understand now," Templar said. "If I had to guess, I'd say there was a conflict between this Gifrōren and the dragons in the past. Perhaps they took something from him. Maybe…"

Duncan and Kathy waited for him to continue.

"Mr. T?" Duncan said, after a few moments.

"Sorry, something occurred to me. This Gifrōren, while he may have limited powers, is still a formidable force. Why would he refrain from getting rid of those he takes prisoner? Why keep Kristin all this time? Why would anyone do that?"

The three remained silent, lost in their own thoughts.

"A bargaining chip!" Duncan said. "He kept them for bargaining chip in the event the dragons returned."

"That's it, my boy," Templar said. "He's not trying to stop the dragon's return. He wants something they took from him, and we need to figure out what that is."

"That makes sense," Kathy said. "Once they learned the eggs had arrived, they went after Destiny and the nest. They are the ultimate bargaining chips.

"Maybe we don't need to become his prisoners to defeat him. Maybe we need to become his ally. Much easier to have him with us than against us."

"But why would he ever join us?' Duncan said. "He's done nothing but try to stop us."

"Think about it, Duncan," Templar said. "What he's done is try to get to the eggs. His methods may not have been pleasant, but he's never actually hurt any of us. Threaten, yes. Harm, no."

"So, are we just supposed to go find him and say, 'Hey there, Mr. Gifrōren, wanna be our friend?"

"Not quite that simple, Duncan," Kathy said. "We need to find out what he's after from the dragons. If we find that, we have our own bargaining chip."

Chapter 48   The Enemy of My Enemy…

"Now what do we do?" Duncan said, sitting next to Destiny. "We haven't much time, some of these eggs are moving. They'll be hatching soon.

"Destiny won't be alone anymore."

"Duncan!" Kathy yelled, "Oh, Duncan, you've done it again," she reached over and hugged him.

Duncan chuckled. "I'm getting pretty good at this coming up with stuff out of thin air I guess."

"What are you on about there, Kathy?" Templar said.

"What would be the worst thing in the world for anyone, any creature in the universe?"

Duncan shrugged. Templar put his arms out, his palms up.

"To be alone," Kathy said. "No one wants to be alone."

"And the Gifrōren is alone!" Duncan said. "The dragons of the past must have taken another Gifrōren from him. Or they took something that would become another Gifrōren."

"I bet whatever it was it had some sort of jewels embedded in it, diamonds or rubies," Kathy said. "And, as you well know from the dragon history, it was this desire for control of diamonds and gold that caused the problem in the first place."

"Or maybe it was something else," Duncan said.

"What?" Kathy asked.

"Maybe this Gifrōren has a talent the dragons wanted. Maybe it's not that the Gifrōren had jewels, maybe it can find them."

"I think you're onto something, my boy," Templar said. "All these years the Gifrōren's been searching for his companion."

"Wow, this Gifrōren has been waiting a long time."

"How long would you wait for someone you loved?" Kathy said.

Duncan nodded, blushing. "How do we let him know we know?" Duncan asked.

"We get him to come to us," Kathy said. "Time to let them see Kristin and know Destiny and the eggs are here."

"I'll go get her," Kathy said, "fill her in on things."
*****

"And that's it?" Kristin said, "he's looking for someone?"

"We think so?" Kathy said.

"You know," Kristin said, "now that I think about it, sometimes the Gifrōren would just stand at the entrance of the cave and make this strange noise.

"First, I thought it was some sort of a warning to others to stay away. But it was almost sad in its tone. I can't explain it, but I came to think of it as calling out to another Gifrōren."

"It was, and now we have to let him know we know."

"I can do that," Kristin said.

"How?"

"I spoke with him often. I was there a long time, and he was all I had. It wasn't much, but we did talk. Thinking about it now, he never threatened to harm me. I tried to talk him into letting me go, I knew I wasn't the Dragon Seeker, I think he realized it too, but he just ignored me.

"He didn't know what to do with me. So, he just left me there."

"Maybe he needed you just to have someone to talk to?" Kathy said.

Kristin nodded. "Maybe. Who knows?"

"Ready?" Kathy said. "I don't think they'll come after us right away. They'll send someone back to check on the nest. Once they know we have it, then they'll do something."

Kristin reached for the sliding door handle. "Let's go ruin their day," and climbed out.

Chapter 49   A Change of Tides

"What's this?" the Manticore said, turning to the Gifrōren. "I thought you had them secured? How'd she get back here?"

The Gifrōren studied the scene. "Remain here and keep an eye on them." He motioned for Jamie to come closer. "Do not make the mistake of thinking this is your chance to escape. You'll stay here until I tell you otherwise, understand?"

Jamie nodded. "Hey, I told you, I'm not with them anymore.

"Yes, you said that, but I am not convinced you mean it." He turned to face the Manticore.

"I'll return to my time and see what's happened." The Gifrōren started to fade, "Do not do anything until I return, understand?" then disappeared.

Once the Gifrōren was gone, the Manticore whispered to the Raven Queen. "Who's he to tell us what to do? He lost them, we don't need him anymore.

"I bet they're all in there, nest and all. I say we take them for ourselves. Between us and the Red Dragon we can eliminate the Gifrōren."

The Raven Queen nodded. "I'll go find the Red Dragon. We meet back here in an hour. I'll post my ravens all around the school, you keep on eye here." She pointed at Jamie. "And him?"

"I'll deal with him," the Manticore said. "I owe Mr. Jamieson a little payback for his past transgressions. No worries. By the time you get back, he'll be just a bad memory."

The Raven Queen let out a loud Caw! Caw! and with that, she was off.

*****

"Well," Templar said, peeking out the blind in his office window, "now they know Kristin's here, soon enough they'll know the nest is here as well. I can see ravens all around the school.

"We are quite surrounded."

Duncan rolled to the window. Looking out he could see Jamie facing the Manticore. "What's he doing?" Duncan said.

Templar joined him at the window. "Hmm, it would seem the others have left, likely to bring in more forces. But that look on the Manticore's face seems less friendly. Jamie has a bit of a problem."

"I need to go help him," Duncan said, heading toward the door.

"Wait, Duncan," Kathy said. "Jamie's managed to survive this far, let's see what happens first. They may be trying to draw us out."

Duncan hesitated, then spun his chair around, rolling back to the window. "The hippogriff, Jamie," Duncan said softly. "Ask the hippogriff."

Some friends have such a strong connection, verbal communication is unnecessary. And the hippogriff appearing next to Jamie was pretty convincing evidence.

"You have a true friend there, Duncan," Templar said. "I am convinced he hears what you think."

"We're about to find out if it helps, Mr. T."

*****

"Hello, Jamie," the hippogriff said, "is this annoyance creating problems for you?"

The Manticore smiled. "Be gone, beast. I know you won't do anything more than offer suggestions. Why waste the time?"

The hippogriff rose to her full height, towering over the Manticore. "It's true my kind chose not to interfere with these matters. But you might be surprised what good advice can accomplish." She smiled then walked over to Jamie, whispering in his ear.

"Really?" Jamie said. "That simple?"

The hippogriff nodded, then sat back to watch.

"This is pathetic," the Manticore said, "such silly games."

Jamie stepped forward and the look in the Manticore's eyes said it all.

Another step. Uncertainty now appeared in the widening eyes of the Manticore.

Another step. The Manticore retreated. "One more step and it will be your last, Mr. Jamieson. You little show doesn't bother me."

"One, huh?" Jamie said, then lunged at the Manticore. The startled beast stumbled backwards, regained his footing, then fled to avoid Jamie's persistent advance. He was last seen disappearing into the woods.

Several ravens flew in to attack Jamie, but the hippogriff batted them away. The rest stayed put.

"I can't believe that worked," Jamie said.

"Why not?" the hippogriff said. "There is no more irresistible force than fear and uncertainty. Creatures like that depend on others being afraid of them.

"Inject a little doubt into the mix, a sudden appearance of aggressive resistance, and you've won the battle before it is even fought."

"Where'd he go?" Jamie asked, glancing around.

"Not sure, precisely," the hippogriff said, "but he won't be gone long. Let's get back to the school."

Chapter 50   Where Angels Fear to Tread

"No, absolutely not. No way. Not gonna happen."

Kathy's angry voice echoed off the walls as Jamie and the hippogriff walked in.

"What's going on here?" Jamie said. "I leave you alone for five minutes…"

"Jamie!" Duncan shouted, rolling over to him and over his foot.

"Ouch, hey! I really missed that part," Jamie said, hopping on one foot. "What's all the arguing about?"

"Nothing," Kathy said. "It's all settled," she folded her arms and leaned back against the wall.

"No, it's not!" Kristin said. "You don't get to tell me what to do anymore. My going back there to confront the Gifrōren is the only thing that makes sense. Myrrdin, tell her this needs to be done."

"Tell her she's not going," Kathy said, staring at her sister.

Templar forced a smile, then started to pace. "Yes, ah, well while I see your point…"

"You agree with her?" Kathy interrupted. "You think going back to where she was imprisoned all these years is wise?"

"I didn't say it was wise," Templar said, glancing at Kristin, "but I do think the idea has merit."

Kathy started to object.

"We are engaged in a dangerous effort," Templar said. "Hear me out on this."

Kathy threw her hands up and leaned back on the wall.

"Everything we now believe about the Gifrōren makes sense. While I'm certain it wasn't a pleasant experience, the fact remains that the Gifrōren kept Kristin alive, even after he found out she was not the Dragon Seeker.

"I can conclude one thing from this, there is something fundamentally good within him. He's not seeking to control the dragons; he wants to persuade them to return whatever it is the dragons took from him in the past. He knows they share a collective memory."

"Can I ask something?" Duncan said.

"Please do," Templar said.

"Wouldn't Balinor have known what was taken from the Gifrōren? Why didn't he share that with us?"

"A good question, and I'm not certain about this but during the wars between man and the dragon, some creatures were caught up in the battles without their consent.

"They were forced to choose sides just to survive. If the dragons seized something from the Gifrōren during that time, it may never have occurred to Balinor the creature was an unwilling ally of men. All of that knowledge came with hindsight."

"Wouldn't Destiny know what was taken?" Duncan asked.

The others were stunned into silence.

"What?" Duncan said, "that never occurred to anyone? Remember another of your many favorite sayings, Mr. T? If you don't ask the question, the answer is no."

"Let's ask her," Templar said, leading the band back to the boiler room.

Destiny lay curled up around her eggs. Duncan knew that some had moved. The dragons within shifting positions before starting the hatching process.

"It's getting closer, I'm gonna have to stay here now."

"So, ask her, Duncan," Templar said, "and then we'll leave you alone with her."

Duncan slid into the nest, the magic taking hold, and he put his arm around Destiny.

"You have a question, Donnchadh Ealdgneat?" Destiny's voice echoed in his mind. No one else could hear her.

"I do, Destiny. The Gifrōren seeks something from the dragon. Do you know what it is?"

Destiny's head nodded once, and a tear fell from her eye.

"What is it, my friend, what troubles you?"

"I've remained silent all this time, living with the memories of things dragons have done in the past. I was ashamed to be part of it."

"Those things were done by others; you bear no responsibility for them. And now, perhaps, you can make amends for those past evils. Do you know why the Gifrōren acts as he does?"

"Before the war began, man had taken the Gifrōren's orb which held his child."

"Why?" Duncan asked.

"Because the Gifrōren is connected to the earth. It senses all that is contained in the ground. It can sense diamonds and gold. When men and the dragon became aware of this ability, they both sought to form an alliance.

The Gifrōren put no value in any of these things and refused to help them.

"Several of the men saw the Gifrōren caring for the orb and decided to steal it."

"So, why is he coming after you?"

"When the battle began, the Gifrōren went to the camp built by men. He was there seeking to free his yet unborn child, and he wasn't alone."

"No? Who was he with?" Duncan said.

"The child's mother."

"What happened?"

"He found the orb and the men tried to convince him to join with them against the dragon. The Gifrōren refused, but before he could flee the camp, the dragons attacked.

"Weakened from being away from his home, the Gifrōren and his partner tried to protect the orb. The mother was killed in the attack and the Gifrōren injured.

"When the dragons found the orb beneath the body of its mother, they took it and hid it away."

"Do you know where they hid this orb?"

Destiny nodded. "It is within the old dragon vault. Guarded by the Red Dragon. I do not know where it is."

"So why doesn't this Red Dragon just take this orb and let it hatch?"

"Because powerful magic seals the vault. No dragon can undo the magic used to seal it, so it cannot be opened."

"So, sending Kristin back to contact the Gifrōren won't help?"

"Oh, but it will," Destiny said.

"How?"

"The Gifrōren knows the magic to open the vault, but he doesn't know where it is. Kristin may have the key to finding it and, with the Gifrōren's help, how to open it."

"Oh boy, Kathy is not going to like this?" Duncan said aloud.

"Kathy's not going to like what?" Kathy said.

"Wait, you heard that?"

"I'm not deaf, you know. Are you gonna talk to Destiny or what?"

"I already did," Duncan said.

"How? You've just been sitting there this whole time."

"No, he hasn't, Kathy," Templar said, "they were engaged in quite the conversation, weren't you, my boy?"

"Oh yeah. Okay, listen…" Duncan explained the whole story. "And so, like it or not, Kristin going back there makes the most sense."

Kathy started to speak, then stopped. Kristin put her arm around her.

"Kathy, we all have our part to play in this. Some of it is dangerous, but necessary. This is my part. It's what I've been destined to do."

"I know," Kathy said, "but I don't want to lose you again. It was all my fault."

"No, it wasn't," Kristin said. "It had to happen this way. None of us could have known back then. Everything makes sense now. It unfolded the way it was always supposed to happen."

"She's right, Kathy," Templar said. "Much as I like to think of myself as infallible, the truth is I am not."

"Hey, anybody have a pen and paper?" Jamie asked, causing them all to look at him. "I want to write down this date and time, Mr. T ain't perfect."

Even Templar had to laugh at that.

Chapter 51   Reliving My Worst Nightmare

"I think I should go alone," Kristin said. "Why risk anyone else?'

"I understand, Kristin," Templar said, "but there is strength in numbers. Jamie is resourceful, if a bit challenging, and he has already established a rapport with the Gifrōren, even if it was a bit disingenuous. He's going with you."

"Fine, let's get a move on, those eggs will soon be dragons, and Duncan will need all of us to be back for that."

"Ready?" Templar asked.

Jamie and Kristin nodded.

Templar and Kathy raised their hands over the pair, closed their eyes, and the two vanished.

"I hope we haven't just made a grave error," Kathy said.

"Me too, my dear, me too. Only time will tell.
*****

Standing outside the Gifrōren's cave, Kristin shivered in the cold. "I forgot how cold it was outside here."

"Me too," Jamie said, rubbing his arms and stamping his feet. "Well, ready to meet out fate? At least we'll be warm."

"Have you always been a smartass?" Kristin said.

"Born and bred and proud of it. Follow me." Jamie slid down the slight slope and stood in front of the cave.

It took only a moment for the Gifrōren to appear.

"Can I believe my eyes? Come to rejoin me as a guest with your friend here, Kristin?"

"Not as a guest," Kristin said, "as an ally."

The Gifrōren remained silent for a moment, Jamie sensed he was confused.

"And why would I need such pathetic allies?"

"To recover your child?"

The rage in the Gifrōren was immediate and frightening. "What do you know of this? Do not think you can bargain with me. If you know where the orb is tell me now or you will regret it."

"Please, let me explain," Kristin said.

"Be quick, I have no patience for lies." He turned on Jamie. "As you'll soon learn, Mr. Haworth, for your recent treachery."

"If you want to find your child," Kristin said, "you need to work with us not against us."

"Explain! Now!"

Kristin stepped forward, surprising the Gifrōren. "We know the history. How man stole the orb with your child from you and what happened in the battle.

"We know you only want your orb back and we can help. You may have the magic to open the vault where the dragons concealed the orb. Working together, we can find it."

The delay in the Gifrōren response spoke volumes. He was thinking about the consequences.

"Why should I trust you? How do I know this is not just some attempt to eliminate me?"

"Why would we come here like this?" Kristin said. "It's true, we need your magic to open the vault, but we could just have kept that to ourselves and never looked for the vault, or found our own way in."

Jamie stepped closer. "Listen, I didn't know why you did the things you did. And I would have done anything, including lying to you, to stop you.

"But now I know the truth. You're doing what I would do if someone stole something I love from me. I see what you did in a different light."

The Gifrōren retreated, his eyes switching between Kristin and Jamie. "I already have allies. Why should I listen to you?"

"Yeah, some allies," Jamie said. "The moment you left the Manticore and Raven Queen started making their own plans to get the eggs.

"They're not your allies; they're using you because they're cowards. Once the dragon eggs were in hand, they'd find a way to get rid of you. They are in league with the Red Dragon, and he has what you seek."

The uncertainty was plain on the Gifrōren's face. He didn't know about the Red Dragon working with the others behind his back or that he had his orb.

"Here's something else you didn't know," Kristin said. "It wasn't the attack by man that killed your partner, it was the Red Dragon army."

"No!" the Gifrōren argued. "I saw the arrows that hit her. They were arrows made by men."

"They were arrows made by men, given to the dragons by traitors within the ranks," Kristin said. "They wanted to kill both of you and enslave your child, but things got out of hand."

"Why didn't you tell me this before? You were here a long time."

"We just figured out what happened," Kristin said. "I didn't know it was your child they stole. This history was concealed when the dragons seized to exist."

The Gifrōren furrowed his brow. "But there were some dragons that survived. The Red Dragon for one and a dragon named Balinor."

Kristin nodded. "That is true. One survived, Balinor, to help discover the Dragon Seeker and as guardian of the *LAST* dragon. The other, the Red Dragon, slipped away during the battle, taking your orb with him and concealing it away."

"If the Red Dragon sealed it in the vault, why can't he undo the magic?" the Gifrōren asked.

"Because he didn't seal it. A wizard allied with man saw what happened. He wasn't powerful enough to battle the Red Dragon alone, but he could use magic to seal the vault.

"Over the years, the alliance between the Manticore, Raven Queen, and the Red Dragon, those who wanted enslave the dragons and you child, formed and lay in wait for the Dragon seeker to arrive."

"And I unwittingly helped those responsible for stealing our child," the Gifrōren said.

"You couldn't have known," Jamie said. "Their level of treachery is unfashionable."

"Unfathomable," Kristin corrected him.

"Yeah, that too," Jamie said. "So, what's it gonna be? You with us or not?" Jamie later said he could have sworn he saw a tear and at that moment he knew they'd turned the corner.

The Gifrōren hesitated for the briefest of moments. "Oh, I am with you. If you help find the orb I seek, I shall be forever in your debt."

"Great," Jamie said, "let's get back before I freeze to death."

"Wait," the Gifrōren. "You two go back and protect the dragon and eggs. I shall engage in a little treachery of my own.

"Let these others think we are still in league together and then spring a trap they'll never see coming."

As Jamie and Kristin walked outside, Kristin whispered. "Do you think we can trust him?"

Jame shook his head. "I don't. We'll just have to keep an eye on him."

Chapter 52   Trust is a Tenuous Thing

"So, can we trust him?" Duncan asked, shifting some eggs around to give them room.

"I think we can," Kristin said. "He wants his child back, everything he's done has been to do that."

"What do you think, Jamie?" Templar said.

"About what?" Jamie answered, not looking up from his phone.

"About the price of tea in China!" Templar shouted, then took a deep breath. "Sorry. About our new friend the Gifrōren."

"Oh, yeah, we can trust him. I think I saw him cry when we talked about his kid. Those tears are real, not fake. He wants his kid back."

"From the mouth of babes," Templar said. "Okay, now what happens?"

"Now," Kristin said, "Kathy and I will go try and find the dragon's vault. I think the rest of you should stay here with Destiny.

"By the way those eggs are moving, dragons will be breaking through any minute."

Templar nodded. "I've an idea about where to look. As I recall, from the haze of memory, dragons always favored the south facing slopes of a hill or mountain.

"That's where Duncan found the *LAST* dragon egg and I'll bet the vault isn't far from there."

"Okay," Kristin said, "ready Kathy?"

"Yup, let's go."

"Shouldn't I go with you two?" Jamie said. "You know, as muscle," flexing his arms.

Both young women burst out laughing.

"Hey, I have feelings you know," Jamie said.

"Sorry, Jamie, we, ah, we weren't laughing at you," Kathy said, trying to keep a straight face.

It almost worked until the laughter broke through again.

"Okay, we were laughing at you, sorry. We need that muscle here," Kathy said.

"Yeah," Duncan added, "somebody has to get rid of the shells once the dragons start hatching."

"Everybody is a smartass," Jamie said, flopping down onto the edge of the nest.

Templar pushed the two women toward the door. "Use caution when you leave here. The Manticore may be able to detect any spell you use to conceal your movements."

"How about a diversion?" Jamie perked up, brimming with enthusiasm.

"A diversion?" Templar said.

"Yeah, how about I take one of those bags you used when you came in here, put some junk in it, and go running out the front door?

"Maybe it will draw their attention enough for Kathy and Kristin to slip out unseen."

"Hmm," Templar said, "I'm loathed to admit it, but you may be onto something. And I know how to make it more, shall we say, interesting to them."

"Cool," Jamie said. "What do we do?"

"Go get me one of the bags. Kathy, you and Kristin head to the side door closest to the woods. I'll send Jamie out the other side."

Jamie came back in with one of the large bags.

"Hold it in front of you, my boy. And be ready to close it when I tell you to. You'll have to move fast, ready?"

"Ready," Jamie said, clutching the cinch strings.

Templar closed his eyes, raising his hands over the bag. A swirling, twisting stream of smoke floated from his hands into the bag.

Jamie could feel the bag growing heavier. Then, something inside began writhing, twisting, and pushing on the sides.

"What the…" Jamie said, holding the bag away from his body.

"Close it, Jamie!" Templar said. "You don't want that thing loose in here."

"What the heck is it?"

"A little surprise for the ravens and the others. Something I know about them they do not know I know."

"I hope this bag holds out," Jamie said, a death grip around the top of the bag.

"Once you're outside," Templar said, putting his hand on Jamies shoulder, "and the ravens come to call, open the bag…then run back in here. And I suggest you be quick about it."

Jamie's eyes grew wide. "Quick about opening the bag?"

"No, running."

"Ah, is this safe?"

Templar smiled. "Safe? Probably not. Effective, I believe it will be."

Jamie shook his head. "Okay, what do I do?"

"Hoist the bag up onto your shoulder."

Jamie struggled with the weight and the still moving bag.

"Come on, Jamie," Kathy said, "use those muscles."

Jamie smirked then finally wrangled the bag into position. The shifting weight making him dance to keep it there.

"Okay," Templar said, "we better be quick about this, from the look on Jamie's face, he won't be able to do this for long.

"You two head for the door over there. When you see Jamie head out, give it a few moments then go. Ready?"

The two girls nodded.

"Jamie?"

"Can we just do this? Whatever is in here smells and I'm not gonna be able to hold it much longer."

Templar walked to the door, glanced out the window at the army of ravens, then opened the door.

Jamie ran as best he could, struggling under the shifting burden. Soon as he cleared the door, the ravens were on him.

Templar watched through the window. He had to admire the boy's determination to struggle to the last moment.

Behind him, he heard the other side door close. Let's hope this works, he thought.

Jamie fought his way into the ballfield, then dropped the bag. Ravens dived in, pecking at him and the bag. The Manticore wings beating against the wind reached him and knew he had to move quickly.

Flailing his arms to ward off the ravens, he reached for the tie string and released it. As the bag opened, the biggest snake he had ever seen, or even imagined, slithered out.

Rising almost to the top of the school, the giant hood of the snake blotting out the sun, the snake attacked the ravens. Jamie could sense the panic in the flock.

No longer interested in him, they fled in chaos to avoid the snake.

Jamie started back towards the school. Looking over his shoulder, he could see the snake snapping at the Manticore as it tried to flee the snake's frenzied attack. The Raven Queen, seeing the ferocity of the snake, abandoned her ally and fled.

Ravens littered the ground as the snake's tail slashed them from the sky. Within moments, not a live raven could be seen.

As Jamie made it to the door, Templar ushered him in.

"Nice work, my boy."

"You might have warned me what was in there."

"I thought a surprise would be more enjoyable for you."

"Oh really, thanks for that," Jamie said, brushing raven feathers off his clothes. "What about that snake? You can't just let it roam around out there, people might notice their dogs, cats, and children missing."

"Watch," Templar said, pointing to the window.

Jamie looked out as the snake finished the last of his raven snack. The end of the snake's tail began to smoke and then the entire snake burst into flame, a pile of dark ash in the shape of a snake was all that remained.

"Wow, like those things we get for the 4th of July."

"In a manner of speaking," Templar said. "Now as good a job as you did with the diversion, let's hope Kathy and Kristin can do even better."

Chapter 53   History Lesson

"Look," Kathy said, grabbing Kristin's arm and pointing up.

The Raven Queen and a giant flock of ravens raced back toward the school.

"Whatever Jamie and Myrrdin did, it worked," Kristin said. "

"I think it did," Kathy said, then looked in the direction from where the Raven Queen appeared. "She came from over there, near Diamond Hill. I wonder if that's where the vault is hidden?"

"Myrrdin said it would be close to where Ducan found the egg. But would it be on the same mountain? There's only one there…"

They both knew the answer at the same moment.

"They hid the mountain, not the vault!"

"When you disappeared," Kathy said, "Myrrdin and I had a long time to talk. We tried to figure out how we went wrong about the Dragon Seeker.

"He told me the story of the last battle and how he had been injured by dragon fire. He managed to track the woman who had betrayed the other humans and the dragons and caused the war. She wanted to claim the egg for herself and those loyal to her.

"He knew the only way to save the egg was to hide it with magic so powerful even he couldn't undo it, knowing the Dragon Seeker might someday arise."

"So, Myrrdin hid the mountain?"

"No," Kathy shook her head. "The magic was so powerful and complete even he didn't know how the egg was protected. Only a true dragon seeker would know how to find it."

"Then what is the Red Dragon guarding if no one knows where this vault is?" Kristin said.

"I think the vault, and thus the orb, is hidden by other magic. Dragon magic can be very powerful, but it is not unbreakable. Myrrdin wanted the egg protected, the vault was never part of that. His magic was precise."

"So, we find the Red Dragon, we find the vault?"

"Yup, and the Raven Queen just pointed us to it."

Making their way through the woods, Diamond Hill rose up before them. They went around the base, then began to climb the old ski slope.

"You know, we could fly up there," Kristin said.

"We could, but the magic might draw attention to us and alert the Red Dragon. We can't risk it. Enjoy the walk."

"Great, thanks."

Slogging through the muddy wet grass, suck-stepping through boot-stealing mud, they made it to the top. As Kathy looked back down the path they'd followed, Kristin grabbed her and threw her to the ground.

"What the…"

"Shh!" Kristin said, "look," pointing above them.

The Red Dragon circled the mountain, looking for something.

"Do you think he knows we're here?" Kathy whispered.

"I doubt it," Kristin said. "If he did, he just incinerate us."

"Ah, thanks for that comforting thought," Kathy said, keeping to the shadows of the trees.

The dragon circled once more, then came to land just behind a stand of pine trees.

They could make out movement, but little more.

"We need to get closer," Kathy whispered. "Keep to the shadows and follow me."

They crawled along, taking time between each move to make sure they hadn't been spotted.

"Why is he facing away from Diamond Hill?" Kristin asked. "Wouldn't that be what he needs to watch?"

"It would," Kathy said, "if that is where the vault is hidden. I think there's a whole other mountain there. We can't see it, maybe the dragon can't either, but he knows it's there."

"Why would you think that?" Kristin said, watching the dragon staring at nothing.

"It fits with what Myrrdin remembers from those days. The magic in the sword was very powerful, beyond even his ability to fully understand. The magic hid more than just the dragon egg. It hid an entire mountain with the vault and the orb because the magic understood, even if Myrrdin didn't, that those who wanted the dragon's egg might use the Gifrōren to find it."

Kristin leaned against the white birch, trying to get a better view. Then, she looked at Kathy.

"Hey, don't white birch usually grow in bunches? Stands, I think they're called."

"Yeah," Kathy nodded.

"I wonder…" Kristin said, looking around. There were three white birches lined up in a perfect row. Just past the third birch were two more off to each side at the top of a line of five more birch trees angled away from the line of three.

A perfect disguise, hidden in plain sight.

"It's an arrow," Kristin said, "a white birch arrow pointing to the vault. That's what he was looking for, hard to see here, but to a dragon flying over…"

Kathy stepped back, glanced toward the dragon, then took another step before she saw it.

"You're right, the vault is here. No doubt now."

"Okay, now the real problem. How do we deal with this dragon?" Kristin said.

"Carefully," Kathy said. "Very carefully. Wait, what's that?"

Kristin looked where Kathy pointed, seeing the brief reflection of the sun. But there was nothing there to reflect the light.

"What's catching the light?" Kristin said.

"The most powerful magic in the world is the simplest," Kathy said. "They hid the mountain in plain sight."

"And how did they do that?"

"They didn't make the mountain disappear; they hid the light that reflects off it."

Kristin looked again and caught the briefest of reflections. "For such powerful magic, it seems to be flawed."

"No," Kathy shook her head, "it's not flawed, they just didn't account for time. Everything changes over time, people, dragons, and mountains.

"The mountain changed, and the spell didn't allow for it. That reflection, if I am correct, is the entrance to the vault containing the orb. That's why they tried an alliance with the Gifrōren. I bet the Red Dragon figured it out and put the trees there as a marker."

"I think I can get in there," Kristin said. "I was always good at getting in and out of places."

"Then we need a diversion, something to distract the dragon," Kathy said, "and that would be me."

"You? Is that a good idea?"

"Probably not, but we don't have much choice. If we can get the orb back, the Gifrōren will be firmly on our side. We need all the help we can get.

"Listen, Kristin, getting that orb back is the priority. Let me deal with this dragon. But no matter what happens, find the orb and take it back to the others.

"Don't worry about me, I can take care of myself."

Kristin hesitated for a moment, glancing between the dragon and the tiny reflection, planning her approach.

"Wait," Kathy said, I have an idea. Closing her eyes for a moment, she cleared the mists of memory, returning to the times of the dragon wars. Clasping her hands together, she murmured a few words. Then, opening her hands, an orb appeared.

"Put this in it's place. I don't think they've seen it, and I'm not sure if they'll even look, but if they find a way in like we did, this may fool them long enough so they don't know we've taken it."

Kristin nodded, then took the orb, concealing it in her jacket.

"Okay, draw his attention away. It won't take me but a moment for me to find the gap and get inside. Once you see I am in, you should probably just get away from here.

"Give me some time inside to locate it, then create another distraction, okay? But be careful."

"Careful won't work, but this will," Kathy said.

Before Kristin could react, Kathy darted toward the dragon. It only took a moment for the dragon to sense her movement.

"What's this? The young wizard coming to challenge me? I've destroyed many infinitely more powerful than you, fool."

He turned to face her, the dragon fire beginning to stir within him, the pungent, acrid smell enveloping her.

"Challenge you?" Kathy laughed. "You pose no challenge to me."

The dragon began to rear back.

"Or me," said another Kathy standing behind the dragon.

"Or me," said another and another until there was an army of Kathys facing the dragon.

"Child's play," the dragon said, sending a wall of fire towards several replicas.

The shock on his face when the fire bounced back at him, burning one wing, said it all. She'd won the first round, now came the dangerous part.

*****

Kristin's first instinct was to stay and help, but she knew her responsibility lay elsewhere. Darting behind the dragon, she followed her line of sight to the reflection, quickly finding the entrance.

Slipping inside, the sound of a second volley of dragon fire reached her ears. But she forced herself on.

Moving deeper inside, the cave narrowed the ceiling angling down forcing her to crawl. Rounding a turn, she caught a dull glow coming from just ahead.

First down on all fours, then on her stomach, she fought her way along the sandy ground, the dampness of the walls chilling her. Almost stuck in the tight space, she forced herself to continue.

Panic began to set in, and she had to fight the urge to back away. But the sound of the battle outside spurred her on.

Then she could move no more. The space, too confined for her, seemed to smother her. Slithering back to a wider spot, she decided to try magic.

Just as she began, a voice in her head nagged at her. "If that's all it took to get through, someone would have done it eons ago," the voice warned.

Powerful magic that cannot be undone, Myrrdin had said in telling the story. Magic can't help me, she thought.

A sudden explosion reverberated down the walls and a blast of heat roiled through.

Kathy was battling alone out there; she needed to get to the orb and get out.

Examining the space once more she noticed something odd. The walls were jagged when she first tried to slide past, now they appeared smooth.

Sliding forward, reaching for the wall, the jagged edges reappeared, narrowing the gap. Pulling back, the walls smooth over.

If I can slip by without touching the walls, maybe they'll stay smooth, she thought.

Laying on her back so she could keep an eye on the top and holding her arms tight to her side, she used her heels to push herself inch by inch further in toward the glow.

After several yards, she was exhausted. But then the gap widened, the glow grew brighter, and she found herself able to turn over and get to her knees.

The orb, pulsating blue and green, now within her grasp, was right there. She reached out, then pulled back.

'Too easy," she said to herself. She stared at the orb, uncertainty and fear paralyzing her.

Then she remembered. Myrrdin said powerful but simple. And what can be simpler than using someone's own doubt and uncertainty to protect something?

Let the fears of those who would steal it be the best protection.

She knew what she had to do…

Chapter 54   More than a Legend

Kathy's troop of doppelgangers declined in number with each volley of dragonfire. The dragon learned quickly to reduce the time between attacks to limit Kathy's ability to produce more.

As Kathy dodged another conflagration, she knew her tactics needed to adapt.

Then something occurred to her. The dragon is most dangerous when there is distance between them and their intended target.

Close the gap, reduce the dragon's ability to attack.

Summoning all her power, she did two things. First, she created more duplicates until she felt her power weakening. Then, she charged directly at the dragon surrounded by her army of mirages.

The move caught the dragon by surprise, and he stumbled trying to get airborne. The doppelgangers latched onto the dragon's wings and legs, forcing him to the ground.

Then another thought occurred to her. Something she should have considered *before* launching her attack. Now that she had the element of surprise, and had the dragon on the ground, how would she contain it?

She had a beast infinitely more dangerous than a tiger by the tail and no idea what to do. One thing was certain, the shock of her attack wouldn't last.

*****

Kristin emerged from the vault, orb safely concealed in her backpack, replaced by the decoy.. Smoke and fire engulfed the area, blocking her view.

She sensed movement though the haze but couldn't see.

Her first impulse was to rush forward and find Kathy, but she knew her responsibility lay elsewhere. She needed to return the orb to the Gifrōren before anything else.

It took all her willpower to leave, but she knew Kathy would want her to do nothing less.

*****

Kathy found herself close to the dragon's head, its neck weighed down by two or three of her doubles. As she made her way closer, still uncertain of what she would do, a brief gap is the smoke cleared, and she saw Kristin emerge from the vault.

Fearful the dragon would see Kristin too, Kathy forced herself to move faster. As she closed on the dragon's head, its eyes locked onto her.

"So, wizard, you've decided to make this personal I see. You are weak because you are willing to sacrifice yourself for the greater good. That's your mistake. I have no such notions, or reservations, about what I need to do."

Shaking off the others, and grasping at Kathy with his claw, he rose from the ground.

Rising high into the sky, holding Kathy for the whole world to see, he let out a thunderous roar knowing the others would know what was about to happen.

Kristin, now halfway back to the school, heard the noise and turned to see the dragon and Kathy hovering in the air.

"Noooo!" she yelled and began to turn back, but a firm hand caught her shoulder. Myrrdin Templar held her back.

"Kristin, Kristin, "he said, as she struggled to get free. "Kathy understood it might come to this; you must return the orb, she must face the dragon. What happens now is out of our hands."

Kristin pulled away, tears in her eyes. "I can't let her go. I can't let her go," she sobbed.

Templar put his arm around the girl, hugging her to him. "That's just what Kathy said, when we believed we'd lost you, my dear.

"I don't know what will happen next, but I do know we have to let Kathy do what she set out to do…and so do you." He drew her in one more time.

"Now bring the orb to the Gifrōren, I'll see what I can do here."

"Or I will," the voice of the Gifrōren reached them as it appeared besides them. "You have my orb?" he said, looking at Kristin.

Kristin reached into her bag and pulled out the pulsating orb, handing it to the Gifrōren.

After a few moments, the Gifrōren approached Myrrdin.

"Wizard, are you familiar with the legend of the transformation?"

Myrrdin's eyes widened. "I have heard the story, but I believed it to be just that, a legend."

"It is not," the Gifrōren said. "It is a true. And I am the one whom the story describes. Can you do what is required?"

Myrrdin stared for a moment. "I know what the legend tells us. And I know the process. But this is not something I have ever done. Nor do I believe myself capable of such magic. I fear too much can go wrong."

The Gifrōren held up the orb. "Within this orb lies more hope for the dragon. For that to happen, a wizard such as yourself must perform the transformation.

"I have lost almost everything dear to me in this quest to find my son. Whatever happens is our destiny, something my son and I will face together. I accept that." He held up the orb, "we accept that. I need you to try."

Myrrdin closed his eyes and his long history in this world flashed before him. This was his moment to rise to the occasion as he had asked so many others to do in the past.

Opening his eyes, he nodded but said not a word. Placing his hands together, he began to chant and walk around the Gifrōren.

Placing one foot in front of the other, the rhythmic chant barely audible to Kristin, he paced around the Gifrōren as it caressed the orb.

Later, when they told the story, both Kristin and Myrrdin would tell of a transformation taking place right before their eyes.

In the exact spot where the Gifrōren once held the orb, now stood two Blue-Green dragons.

Kristin leaned over to Templar. "I thought all these dragons were destroyed?"

"So did I, my dear, so did I."

The larger of the two dragons approached them, giving them a slight bow.

"I am Gesselring and this is my son, Gesselroot. We were long imprisoned by the Red Dragon and transformed into Gifrōren. They enslaved us to search for gold and diamonds.

"When the war between the factions of men and dragons began, we tried to escape but the Red Dragon stole the orb that held my unborn son.

"His mother and I searched all the earth to find him. On one such search, we found the orb but the Red Dragon killed my beloved. I vowed to avenge her death once I found my son.

"The legend, of a long-imprisoned dragon and a wizard of destiny, now comes to pass."

The roar of the Red Dragon interrupted their conversation. Still holding Kathy aloft, he shot fire down upon them.

"You and Kristin return to the nest. The eggs are hatching, and the dragon seeker will need help." Gesselring said. "My son and I will deal with this Red Dragon. I've dreamed of this moment forever."

"No!" Kristin said, "I've done my part. The orb is restored. I won't leave my sister."

Myrrdin started to argue, then stopped. Sometimes people need to be free to make their own choices.

"I'll get back to Duncan," he turned to face Kristin. "You get Kathy and come back to us, okay?"

Kristin nodded. "We will…" she focused her gaze on the hovering dragon, "or die trying."

"Yes," Myrrdin said. "Try to avoid that extreme, okay?"

Chapter 55   Fight Fire with…Courage

Kristin, Gesselring, and Gesselroot gathered beneath an overhanging cliff. The Red Dragon made passes overhead, scorching ground with each pass.

"How are we going to get to her without him hurting her, or worse?" Kristin asked.

Gesselring peeked out from under the cliff, catching a glimpse as the dragon flew overhead.

"I'm not sure we can, even though there's three of us, we can't get close enough, fast enough, to stop him."

"How about we rush him all at once? Maybe he'll drop her, then I can grab her," Kristin said.

"And if you miss?" Gesselring asked.

"I won't."

"I don't know, Kristin, too many things can go wrong here," Gesselring said, ducking as another volley of fire scorched the ground.

Then, as the trio tried to decide what to do, the Red Dragon chose for them.

"Enough of this nonsense," the Red Dragon said, landing a short distance away. He tossed Kathy to the ground, then placed his foot squarely on top of her.

"Perhaps a little squashed bug for a sister might make your day," the dragon said, applying more force.

Kathy let out a scream as the pain intensified.

Kristin rushed from their hiding spot, trying to invoke powerful magic that would drive the dragon back.

It didn't work.

The dragon reared back, ready to launch dragon fire.

Gesselring turned to his son. "This is your moment, son. My time is at an end. Remember why we are put into this world, to care for others. Never forget that. Do what you can to help them save the dragons."

Before Gesselroot could answer, his father embraced him then flew toward the Red Dragon.

The sudden appearance of the blue-green dragon, the mortal enemy of the Red Dragon, had its effect. The Red Dragon reeled back, lifting his foot off Kathy, turning to face the threat.

Kristin and Gesselroot charged forward, grabbing the badly injured Kathy and dragging her away.

"Take her back to the others," Gesselroot said. "I will stay with my father."

"But he said…"

Gesselroot cut her off. "I know what he said, and I know what I must do. Go, protect her, and return to the nest. Your fight is now ours."

Gesselring flew straight at the eyes of the Red Dragon and unleashed a wall of dragon fire, partially blinding him. Misjudging the distance, Gesselring couldn't stop his forward momentum, and he crashed into the now howling Red Dragon.

The force of the impact knocked the Red Dragon to the ground. The two dragons fighting to gain control. They struggled back to their feet.

The Red Dragon, unable to see but still a powerful and dangerous creature, tried to pry himself away from Gesselring, but the blue-green dragon held tight to the Red Dragon's wings.

Locked into a deadly embrace, neither able to break the other's grip, they disintegrated into giant ball of dragon fire.

Chapter 56   The Nature of Dragons

Kristin, Jamie, and Templar all huddled around the nest. Duncan, floating gently in the air just above the middle, was surrounded by small versions of Destiny, ninety-eight at the final count, turns out dragon eggs can hold twins. The baby dragons all crawling and pawing at Duncan to get his attention.

Destiny slept soundly, several of the baby dragons cuddled up next to her. A roaring fire in the fireplace warmed the room and cast flickering shadows everywhere.

Keladry came in from the back into the main room, wiping her hands on a towel. "I see everyone has settled in. Moving the nest here was wise, Myrrdin. We can guard them better."

Templar nodded. "How's the patient?"

Keladry's face grew concerned.

Kristin blanched at the sight.

"She's fine, Kristin, fine," Keladry said. "She's finally asleep."

"She'll be okay?" Kristin asked.

Keladry folded the towel and placed it on the table. She took a deep breath, looking at each of the anxious faces watching her.

"I won't lie to you. She suffered serious injuries. When a Red dragon attacks an enemy, they use a combination of force, fire, and venom.

"In this case, she was almost immersed in it. But she knew enough to avoid breathing it in. I don't know how, but she did.

"Her injuries are severe, broken arm, severe laceration of one leg, multiple broken ribs, but they will heal," she gathered her thoughts.

"And the poison?" Kristin said. "You have an antidote, right?"

Keladry shook her head. "I'm afraid it is not that simple. Dragon venom is insidious in nature. While it acts in the same way generally, it has characteristics designed to counteract antidotes.

"What might work well in one case, could prove fatal in another. I'm not sure what I am facing here so finding the antidote is challenging."

"What do we do?" Kristin asked.

"The hardest thing," Keladry said. "We wait. Kathy understood the nature of dragons. I believe she took precautions before she exposed herself to the Red Dragon.

"Since not knowing the particular nature of the toxin, anything I do would be a guess, just as likely to harm her as to heal her." She walked over to Kristin, putting her hand on her shoulder.

"We have to rely on Kathy to find her way back to us."

"And what if you're wrong," Kristin said, pulling away, her voice rising and tears falling. "We can't just wait around and watch her die! I won't do that. There has to be something we can do." She ran from the room, slamming open the door to the outside.

Jamie started after her.

"Wait, Jamie," Templar said, holding him back. "Give her time. She knows Keladry is right. It's the despair of being unable to do anything driving her anger.

"She'll be back."

Jamie looked at the door for a moment, then went back to stand next to the nest.

"Duncan," Templar said, "what do you think?"

Lifting several of the small dragons off himself, he floated to the edge of the nest.

"As hard as it is, I now know this is where I need to be. Kathy would not want us to do anything to jeopardize these dragons.

"Magic draws attention. The ones who want to destroy or control the dragons know what happened to her. They'll be looking for signs of any effort to find an antidote.

"My first instinct is to hunt them down and force them to give us the cure. But that's what they'd want us to do, and it would risk their discovering where we are.

"We have to put our trust in Kathy, it's what she would expect from us."

"I hope you're right, Duncan," Kristin said, surprising them as no one heard her return. "And I hope we can all live with that choice…if we're wrong."

*****

"Duncan," Destiny's voice reached into his mind. "Did it never occur to you to ask me what to do? I am a dragon after all."

"I know," Duncan answered, "but you're not a Red dragon."

"But I am a dragon and thus capable of finding the antidote."

"How?" Duncan asked.

"You must trust me to do this. You care for these dragons, and I will seek the antidote."

"But we can't risk losing you."

"Duncan, life is a series of risks. One cannot live without there being challenges. If there were no risks there'd be no reward.

"Every moment of life comes with risk. But it also comes with the opportunity to experience joy, love, hope, laughter, friendship, accomplishment, and purpose.

"Life may not be fair but what is the alternative? You and Kathy and the others risked everything for me and my children, I can offer the same in return.

"Let me be the one accepting risk for a change. But you have to let me go. I cannot go without your consent."

"Why do you need my consent?" Duncan asked.

"Because I am indebted to you for saving me."

Duncan thought for a long moment, fearful of the choice before him.

"I don't want to lose you, and there is much to do before the dragon is restored, but perhaps we all must accept risk in achieving our goal."

Destiny bowed her head. "You are wise beyond your years, dragon seeker. To understand such matters is no small feat. So, what shall it be, Duncan?"

Duncan glanced around the room, the others all watched, sensing he was communicating with Destiny. They knew this was between him and her alone.

"Go," Duncan said aloud, "Find the antidote and bring it back to us."

Before anyone in the room could react, Destiny unfolded her wings, jumped from the nest, moved to the open door, and flew off.

"Where's she going?" Jamie said. "Shouldn't she stay here with these guys?" gesturing toward the mass of baby dragons jostling to look for their mother.

"She's living up to her name," Templar said. "isn't she, Duncan?"

"She is, Mr. T, she is."

Chapter 57   But I am No Hero...

"Okay, here's what we do," Duncan said. "We'll work in teams to guard the dragons. Kristin, you and Jamie will take the first watch.

"Keladry and Myrrdin will take the second watch. Try to rest when it's the other team's turn."

"And you, my boy?" Templar said, but the look on his face said he knew the answer.

"I'm going to help Destiny. I know what she's going to do, and I need to be there."

"Alone?" Templar said. "Is that wise?"

Duncan held Templar's gaze. "It is necessary."

"Spoken like a true hero."

"I am no hero, Mr. T, but I am the dragon seeker, and I will not lose one more friend in this quest."

*****

Sliding back into his chair, he made his way back to the school. Exhausted from the effort, he willed himself to climb into the OHRV they'd hidden there.

Pulling his chair in next to him, he hoped he could remember how to control this thing. Reaching for the starter, he hesitated for a moment, hand shaking.

Then a sound reached his ear. Soft, indistinguishable at first, then growing in intensity. A scream. An anguished tormented scream of agony reaching into the depths of his mind. The voice familiar, sending a sense of rage through him.

Destiny was in trouble.

Punching the starter button, stomping on the accelerator, the OHRV shot into the sky, weaving and bouncing as Duncan tried to maintain control.

Turning north, he knew where he needed to go.

Chapter 58   Sometime There Is No Choice

Circling over Diamond Hill, Duncan could see the manticore surrounded by thousands of ravens. The Raven Queen was nowhere to be seen, but she wouldn't be far.

Taking the OHRV lower, his heart almost stopped beating. There, on the ground in front of the manticore, was Destiny.

Caution fled from his mind, and he dove down, bringing the OHRV to land. Driving directly at the manticore, his approach announced by a chorus of screeching ravens.

"And just like clockwork, the would-be hero arrives," the manticore said. "Come to join your friend in leaving this world?"

"Let her go, it's me you want. I am the Dragon Seeker. I am the one who can restore the dragons."

"My, my," the manticore hissed, "aren't we full of ourselves. I think I'll let both of you suffer a bit until you give me the rest of the dragons. They must all be hatched by now or this one," pressing down on Destiny's neck, "wouldn't have left them."

Pressing one clawed paw harder onto Destiny's neck, she cried out in pain, then struggled out from under him, rushing to Duncan.

"The antidote is in your heart, Duncan. I should have figured it out before. You can save Kathy. I'll deal with this. He can do nothing to me that matters. Go! Save her and the dragons. This is my path; you cannot change it."

The manticore redoubled his effort to silence Destiny, lunging for her, but she proved more resilient, dodging his claws.

"Remember what Balinor said, 'Se Draca álibbend, na des Draca...*The* dragon lives forever, but not *this* dragon.' As it was with him, so it is with me."

Destiny struggled and upended the manticore. She pounced on him, holding him down.

"Go, Duncan, go now. Save Kathy and our dragons. Follow your path and I will follow mine."

"But how?" Duncan said, "what antidote is in my heart?"

Destiny rose to her full height, still struggling to hang onto the manticore. The creatures poison-tipped tail snapping at her, narrowly missing.

"Go to her, Duncan," Destiny said. "You'll understand when you look in her eyes."

Torn by indecision, Duncan didn't know what to do. He couldn't leave Destiny, and he couldn't let Kathy die. Why do these things always come down such choices?

Watching Destiny fight against the manticore, he started to move forward...then Destiny stopped struggling, turned her back to the manticore, and stood still.

The tail snapped back, ready to strike.

"Move, Destiny, move!" Duncan yelled. But she remained frozen in place.

"As is my name, this is the path I choose," Destiny said.

Duncan didn't know which way to move.

Joe Broadmeadow

And then the whipping sound of the tip of the tail striking Destiny decided for him…

Chapter 59   The False Promise of Immortality

"Gone?" Templar said, "What do you mean gone?"

Duncan wiped a tear, looking at the others watching him. "Destiny fought off the manticore. She told me the antidote was in my heart and that I could save Kathy. She…" his voice cracked, "She reminded me what Balinor had said about the dragon lived forever but not…"

"Duncan, tell me what happened," Templar said. "Don't leave anything out."

After Duncan finished the story, Templar remained silent.

"Do you know what Destiny meant by the antidote was in my heart?" Duncan asked.

Templar shook his head. "No, my boy, I don't. That's something you need to figure out."

Duncan's eyes blinked the tears away and he tilted his head. "Then why did you need me to tell you the whole story?"

Templar smiled. "Because there's a chance, albeit a small chance, Destiny is not lost."

"But the manticore's tail carries deadly poison, doesn't it? No one can survive it," Kristin said.

"Usually," Templar said, tapping his chin, "unless…"

"And you think…" Kristin answered but Templar cut her off.

"I think there's a chance she knew what she was doing. Drawing attention to herself to give Duncan time to figure things out.

"But I don't understand," Duncan said. "Why did she have to go if she knew what the antidote was?"

"That's the thing, Duncan," Templar said. "She didn't know until she faced the manticore. Something happened and she figured it out.

"If you hadn't gone to find her, we might never have known."

"Thing is, Mr. T, I still don't know what to do."

"You will, my boy, you will. Destiny bought us time. But if I am right, and there is a chance she knows something about the manticore poison we don't, there's not much time to save her. "

"You think she's alive?" Jamie said.

Templar nodded. "For the moment. Okay, Duncan, put your trust in what Destiny said. You have what it takes to save Kathy within you, go figure out how.

"Jamie," Templar said, turning to the others, "you, Keladry, and I are going to find Destiny. Kristin, you have the dragons, they'll be hungry again soon. You need to keep them quiet, or the ravens may hear them.

"It's only a matter of time before they find us here. We must be prepared to move again."

Templar, Jamie, and Keladry headed out the door. Duncan and Kristin sat in silence for a long moment.

"I have no idea what Destiny meant," Duncan said. "Not a clue."

Kristin walked over, gently pushing one of the more adventurous young dragons back into the nest while the faces of others peered over the edge.

"She said it was in your heart, right?"

Duncan nodded.

"And you needed to look into her eyes?"

"Yup."

"Then do that. Don't think about it, go to her, listen to your heart."

Duncan started to turn his chair, then stopped. "Aren't you coming with me?"

Kristin shook her head. "I want to. I really do, but I can't. This is something only you can do, Duncan. Alone. I'll wait here with the dragons. You need to do this by yourself. But I do know one thing."

"What's that?"

"You must believe you can do this, or it won't work. Destiny couldn't tell you what to do, she had to show you."

Duncan nodded, spun his chair, and wheeled himself into the back room.

A small fire flickered in the fieldstone hearth, dim but still offering warmth. Kathy lay on the bed wrapped in a quilt. Her breathing was shallow but steady. A soft groan rose from her lips as she shifted her position.

Duncan rolled closer, unsure what to do next.

"I know you're there," Kathy said, her voice raspy and but a whisper. "You can come closer, I'm not contagious."

Duncan forced a smile and came to the edge of the bed.

"I heard you talking out there," she shifted back on the pillow, raising her head. A cough followed by another moan brought the reality of her condition back into focus.

"Don't move, Kathy, just rest," Duncan said.

"Don't tell me what to do," Kathy smiled, "I'm not that weak."

"Ah, yes you are," Duncan said.

"Okay, for the moment maybe," Kathy said, her eyes betraying her pain.

"So, what's this about Destiny I heard? She fought with the manticore?"

"She said she was going to find the antidote for the dragon poison in you." Duncan shrugged, "I don't know what happened before I got there, but she told me the antidote was in my heart."

"She did?"

Duncan nodded.

"And is it?"

"I have no idea what she meant. Why would she challenge the manticore is she knew the answer already?"

"Wait, she...let herself...be struck?" Kathy said, struggling to get the words out.

Duncan nodded. "As soon as that happened, I knew it was hopeless so I came back here as fast as I could."

"Or," Kathy said, eyes fluttering closed, "she was showing you the way."

She fell silent.

"Kathy?" Duncan said, "Kathy, KATHY!"

It seemed to Duncan she was no longer breathing. He reached for her free arm, shaking her.

"Kathy, Kathy! Wake Up!"

"Hey, hey" she said, "easy on your dying friend here pal," using humor to mask the pain.

"Duncan, think about this. Destiny said the antidote is in your heart, right?"

"Yeah. And?"

"And what does a heart do?"

"It pumps blood," Duncan said, growing uneasy. "This isn't time for an anatomy lesson."

"You're missing the point," Kathy said, her voice weakening by the moment. "Your blood could be…" and she passed out again.

No matter what he did, he could not get her to wake up. She was breathing, but it was growing weaker and out of rhythm.

"Kathy, come on, my blood could be what? My blood could be…" and the words stopped as the idea formed in his mind.

Looking around, he spotted the small knife on the table next to the bandages Keladry cut from the cloth. Grabbing the knife, he moved to Kathy's side where she'd suffered a leg wound.

Pulling back the bandages, exposing the still seeping wound, Duncan took a deep breath. I hope I'm right about this.

Pulling the knife quickly against his fingertip, he dripped his blood onto the wound.

Nothing happened.

Several more drips fell, smoke rose from where the drops of blood landed, the wound stopped leaking and began to close.

A moment later Kathy woke up.

"…your blood could be…"

"…Dragon's blood," Duncan finished the sentence. "And dragons are immune to their own poison."

Kathy sat up in bed and flexed her leg. Reaching for the splint holding her arm, she pulled it off, waving the now healed arm in the air.

"You're a miracle worker, Duncan," she said, jumping from the bed. "How did you figure it out?"

"Because people always treat me differently, even though I don't feel that way. But when you said something about my blood, I thought, maybe I am different. Maybe I have dragon's blood in me.

"Destiny wanted me to figure it out for myself, so I'd believe it."

"There is no doubt now, you are the dragon seeker. Okay, where is everybody?" Kathy asked.

"Mr. T, Jamie, and Keladry went looking for Destiny. But I'm not sure why. Kristin is with the baby dragons; you should go see her."

The two walked out of the back room and saw Kristin, surrounded by baby dragons, sleeping soundly.

"Watch this," Kathy said, winking. She crept closer to the nest, then ducked down. In an amazing similar voice to Mr. T, she yelled, "Why are you sleeping?"

Kristin shot up, her head on a swivel looking for Templar. Then she heard Kathy's giggle.

"You scared the…wait you're alive!," falling out of the nest to hug Kathy.

"You sound surprised," Kathy said. "Did you expect me to die?"

"Yes. I mean no. I mean what happened? Keladry made it sound like you were a goner."

"Duncan happened. He figured out he has dragon blood, and it counteracted the poison."

"Brilliant. Okay, now what do we do?" Kristin said, still holding Kathy's hand.

"Duncan, I know why Mr. T took the others to find Destiny."

"It's not to find her body, is it?" Duncan said, his look fearing the answer.

"I don't think so," Kathy said. "I'm not certain of this, there are so many thinks about dragons we don't know, but I'm betting Destiny may be at least resistant, if not immune, to most poisons. Even those from a manticore.

"If I'm right, her whole purpose was to buy you time to figure it out once she understood the truth. She believed you'd see her courage as inspiration. She was uncertain but accepted the risk. She hoped you would as well."

"I still don't understand why people can't just tell me these things," Duncan said. "Everything has to be a riddle."

"The most important truths are those we discover for ourselves.," Kathy said. "Almost everything you've done these last few months you did because you learned them on your own.

"That is the way of the world, Duncan. Especially your world."

Several of the baby dragons, awakened by all the commotion, decided now would be the time to test their wings.

Jumping off the edge of the nest, one flew into Duncan's lap, another bounced off Kathy, crashing to the floor.

"Oh great," Duncan said, "they go right from hatching to flying. How are we ever going to control them?"

As the words came out, two more, inspired by their brothers and sisters, joined the chaos. Soon, the entire room was flooded with small flying dragons crashing into walls and bouncing off each other.

Duncan covered his head with his hands, Kathy and Kristin hid under the table.

"How are we gonna stop them?" Duncan said, as two more landed on his lap.

"I have no idea," Kristin said. "You're the dragon seeker, you do something."

"How am I supposed to do that?" Duncan said, pushing the dragons away.

The two girls stared at him.

"Oh yeah, figure it out, Duncan. Use your head, Duncan. Of course, you can do it, Duncan."

One of the baby dragons landed on the edge of his wheelchair, staring at Duncan.

"Bistu thēo, ther draco suohhit? (Are you the one that seeks the dragon?)"

"Kehre jetzt zum Nest zurück! (Return to the nest now!)," Duncan replied.

Like magic, all the dragons returned to the nest, lined up on the edge, and waited for the next command.

Duncan blinked at them.

"Where did that come from?" Kathy asked.

"I have no idea," Duncan said.

"Waz ist unsēr muoter, Tracho fāheri? (Where is our mother, Dragon Seeker?)"

"Reht hiar, niowiht wīhs wīrs giwesan (right here, none the worse for wear)," Templar said, leading the way into the room followed by an injured, but very much alive, Destiny, and the others.

"I didn't know you and Duncan spoke dragon," Kathy said.

"I didn't know I spoke dragon," Duncan said. "I know phrases Balinor taught me, but that's it."

"It's not strictly Dragon," Templar said. "Closer to Old High German in a way. It's a wizard thing. Your tongue would tie itself in a Gordian knot if you even tried Dragon language. This is a happy medium." He smiled as Destiny flew into the nest and was surrounded by her children.

"So, what happened to the manticore?" Duncan said.

"He was gone when we got there," Jamie said. "We saw Destiny collapsed on the ground. We thought she was dead, apparently so did the manticore."

Templar picked up the story. "As I got closer, something about what Destiny had told you, Duncan, gnawed at me. Then, I realized what she had done."

"What?" Duncan said, rolling to the nest and stroking Destiny's neck.

"She believed her dragon blood would be enough to tolerate the manticore poison. She was right, although the poison did weaken her. But I think she'll fully recover."

Duncan remained silent for a moment.

"What is it, Duncan?" Kathy said. "What's wrong."

"Something's not right. I get what Destiny did and why. But the manticore just leaving her when he wasn't certain he'd killed her doesn't make sense.

"Why not take the body and use it as a bargaining chip? We didn't know if she was dead or alive. If we thought they had her, we'd do everything to get her back.

"It doesn't make sense…"

The rumbling started slowly at first, like a long, rumbling thunderclap, then exploded into a cacophony of shrieking ravens, smoke, and darkness.

Then everything went dark.

Duncan opened his eyes, his view of the inside sideways from normal. He realized he was lying on the floor. His wheelchair was upside down on top of him. His brain unable to reconcile what was happening.

Templar, sitting with his back against the wall, held his head, shaking it to clear the effect of the concussion.

Keladry and the others struggled to stand.

Duncan pulled himself to the sitting position, turned his chair upright, and struggled into it.

Kathy helped Kristin and Keldary, while Duncan went to Templar.

"You okay, Mr. T? You look like someone knocked the stuffing out of you."

"I'll be okay," Templar said. "Just help me up."

As the smoke and dust settled, the horror of the moment struck them all.

Jamie, Destiny, and all the dragons were gone.

Chapter 60   A Trojan Dragon

"What happened?" Kathy said. "How did they know? How did they find us?"

"A trojan dragon," Duncan said. "That's why they left Destiny for you to find. Somehow, they tracked her back here. I should have known."

"No, my boy, this is on me," Templar said. "In our joy at finding Destiny alive we forgot who we are dealing with.

"The problem now is how do we find them?"

"The beginning," Duncan said. "We go back to where this all started."

"What do you mean, Duncan?" Templar said.

"They want to control the dragon or, if they can't so that, they'll destroy them. Diamond Hill is where I found Destiny. It is there the magic of the dragon is centered. If they can control that, they can alter the future of the dragon.

"We'll find them there."

"But they'll expect us to come there," Kathy said. "And they won't welcome the visit."

"True," Duncan said. "But what they can't be certain of is whether they can succeed without me. They know they can't care for the dragons alone. Destiny brought them into the world, but I think it will take both of us to fully raise them.

"They need me to cooperate and that's why they took Jamie."

"We need to keep you safe, Duncan," Kathy said," and not let them near you."

Duncan shook his head. "No, it's too late for that. They won't wait. If they can't gain control, they'll start disposing of the dragons.

"There is no safe place for me if we want to save the dragons. I need to go there."

"And do what?" Kristin said, "sacrifice yourself? What can you do against all of them?"

"What I have been doing since this whole thing began. Figuring it out."

Duncan rolled over to the fireplace mantle, removing one of the stones. Hidden within, the egg he had selected as the new LAST dragon shimmered in the firelight.

"Destiny and I selected this as the LAST Dragon. Even if all else fails, this cannot be lost. Mr. T, you need to work your magic again and hide this egg. Take the others with you, I'll follow my own destiny and go to Diamond Hill."

"No way," Kathy said. "No way you're going alone. The others can hide the LAST Dragon, I'm going with you."

"But I have to…"

Kathy cut him off. "There is no debate here, I have devoted my existence to your success and nothing, absolutely nothing, is going to change that. Save your breath."

Duncan looked at Templar.

"She's serious, my boy. And she is right. We will take the LAST Dragon and conceal it. We will be as quick as we can and come to join you." Templar put his hands on the Duncan's shoulders.

"While I feared it might come to this, I harbored a slight hope it would not. I cannot do anything else; it is all in your hands. Follow your heart and may the power and legacy of the dragon go with you."

Reaching for the wall, he removed the egg and wrapped it in his cloak. He nodded at Duncan, then turned away. A tear fell from his eye as he made his way to the door. The others followed in silence.

"It's just you and I, Duncan," Kathy said.

"You sure about this, Kathy?"

"I've never been more certain in my entire life."

Chapter 61   A Debt Repaid

Kathy and Duncan peered through the underbrush at the gathering of enemies.

The Manticore, Raven Queen and her army, and a burned and bruised but very much alive Red Dragon surrounded Destiny and the dragons.

Destiny stood defiantly at the nest, holding those around her at bay with the threat of dragon fire. The baby dragons huddled in the nest, unsure of what to do.

Except for two of the bolder ones. They mimicked their mother, striding defiantly on the edge of the nest, trying to be as intimidating as they could.

"How are we gonna take on all of them?" Kathy said.

"Not quite sure yet, it does seem like we're outnumbered," Duncan said.

"Duh, two against several thousand," Kathy said. "Yeah, that sounds a bit unbalanced."

"Four you mean," the other voice catching them by surprise. Kathy and Duncan looked behind them, shocked to see two blue-green dragons sitting on their haunches.

"Who? Ah, are you...?" Kathy said, scrambling back.

"We are indeed. Gesselring and Gesselroot, at your service."

"But I thought you..." Kathy said.

"Yes, it did seem that I was incinerated. But my stubborn son here, who does not know how to follow instructions, decided to stay and intervene.

"Apparently, he learned something about the Red Dragon. He used it to deflect the dragon fire back at the Red Dragon, seriously injuring him but not fatally, I'm afraid. He is very much in the mix, but on a positive note, so are me and my son."

"Glad to hear that," Duncan said, "but with all due respect, doubling our forces isn't much of a gain."

"That is true, Duncan, but as a wise man once said, "every battle is won long before it is fought.'"

Duncan glanced at Kathy then back at Gesselring. "How is that possible?"

"Because once the battle starts, things happen you cannot control. But if one uses their resources to their full advantage, and takes control of the battlefield through careful planning, victory is assured."

"And you have a plan?" Duncan said.

Gesselring shook his head. "No, but at least I know we need one."

Duncan and Kathy both had to smile at that.

"Okay then, let's come up with a plan."

Chapter 62   When All Else Fails, Trust No

One

The manticore hissed at Destiny, kicked at the immobile Jamie, then sidled up to the Red Dragon.

"How long do we keep this up? Let's just dispose of a couple of the scrawnier little ones, that will give her plenty of incentive to cooperate."

"No," said the Red Dragon, "we need the Dragon Seeker for us to have complete control. By now they've hidden another LAST dragon egg. If we don't succeed now, the whole process just starts over.

"I know they are nearby, planning their rescue. We take them all at once, or we get rid of them all at once. Either way they'll be no Dragon Seeker to restore the dragons. We'll have them all in our control…or gone forever."

The Red Dragon locked eyes with Destiny, surprised by her defiance against all odds.

"I will give her this, she has more courage than I anticipated," a smile grew across his face. "Perhaps your little incentive idea has merit. Take some of her determination away."

The speed with which the Red Dragon moved caught them all by surprise. Before anyone could react, he launched himself into the air, swooped over the nest, and snatched one of the small dragons from the huddled mass.

Circling high above the nest, he feigned dropping the little one several times before returning to land. Tossing the terrified, screaming baby to the ground he placed a giant claw on the dragon and squeezed.

The baby cried out in agony.

Destiny was torn. If she left the nest the others would be vulnerable to the ravens and the Manticore. If she stayed, her baby was certain to die.

Making such decisions, where you sacrifice one for the good of the many, is easy in theory but agonizing in practice.

However, the is one thing about dragons, they are a quick study. While this Red Dragon's allegiance against his own was an outlier among the dragon realm, his skills were not unique.

And they were easily mimicked.

One of the more defiant young ones slid off the back of the nest while everyone's attention was on the Red Dragon.

Creeping slowly along, stalking like a lion on the hunt, he waited until he'd come as close to his brother as possible without drawing attention.

Embracing his new found appreciation for surprise, he leapt into the air, flew directly at the eyes of the Red Dragon, and leashed a powerful, if miniaturized, stream of dragonfire, temporarily blinding the Red Dragon.

In agony, the Red Dragon pulled back, releasing the pressure on his captive.

His now emboldened brother swooped down, herding his now free brother back to the nest. Destiny nuzzled the two, lifting them back into the nest, dragging Jamie along with them.

The Red Dragon raged about, one eye seared closed, the other red, teary-eyed, and weakened but still working.

"Enough of this," he roared. Turing to face the woods he yelled. "Dragon Seeker, I know you are there. Show yourself or will incinerate this nest and all these dragons."

The Manticore and Raven Queen pulled back, whispering to each other.

"We can't let him destroy them," the manticore said. "All our efforts will be for naught."

"He won't, and they know that as well as we do," the Raven Queen said. "We need to reassert ourselves. He is powerful but doesn't understand how to manage his power. You remember how we converted him to our cause?"

The manticore nodded.

"I think it's time for us to remind him he needs us if he wants to rule the dragons."

With that, the Raven Queen rose on her wings and flew to the Red Dragon. Gently touching his burns, she drew the pain away.

"Listen my old friend. This is not the time to settle the score. We have our chance to control the dragons but only if we control ourselves.

"The Dragon Seeker will come. Of that there is no doubt. Seek your revenge on him through his friends. Do as you will with them. But keep in mind the goal here.

"And remember, we know the location of the gold and diamond mines, not you. You need us to find them. Once we control the dragons, we control the world. Everything we desire will be ours. That is what we have fought for all these centuries."

The Red Dragon turned away. He knew she was right; he needed them more than they needed him. But he would mark his time. There was no trust here, only a shared goal.

The time would come when the balance of power would shift. Then we'll see who controls things.

"I understand," the Red Dragon said. "We will wait for the Dragon Seeker." Rising to his full height, he towered over the Raven Queen.

"But make no mistake about it, when we capture them, I will decide when and how they will meet their end. Understood?"

The Raven Queen nodded. "Of course, my friend, of course," then flew back to meet the manticore.

"Well?" The Manticore said.

"He is no longer to be trusted."

"I never did anyway," the Manticore answered. "The sooner we get rid of him the better."

Chapter 63   A Time for Everything

It took everything Kathy and Kristin had to stop Duncan from charging into the fray. The sound of the screaming baby dragon infuriated him.

"Duncan, Duncan! Stop," Kathy said, taking him by the shoulders as she blocked his way. "Can't you see this is exactly what they want us to do?"

"But he's just a baby," Duncan said, tears forming in his eyes.

"Duncan, listen to me. There are more than ninety babies there. You'll do none of them any good if you get yourself killed. They need you. Destiny needs you. We all need you."

Duncan slumped back in his chair, resigned to the truth in Kathy's words, but he'd make the Red Dragon pay for what he'd done.

Gesselring and his son motioned for the others to follow them. Moving a safe distance away, father and son turned to face the others.

"Look, the Red Dragon knows nothing of my transformation. As far as we know, he believes the orb to still be hidden.

"I can transform back into my other form and infiltrate them. Get close to them and convince them to let me deal with the nest and Destiny while they deal with you guys."

"But what if they do know?" Gesselroot said. "Then what?"

"Then, my son, the battle will be on. But I don't think that will be the case."

"How will you transform?" Kathy asked. "Templar is the only one who can do this."

Gesselring shook his head. "No, there is someone else with the power to do this among us."

Kathy shook her head, stepping back. "No way, that is way beyond my skills."

"And mine," Kristin added.

"It's not either of you," Gesselring said, turning to Duncan. "It's you, young man. The power to transform is lies within you."

"Me?" Duncan said, "I have no idea how to…" and then a memory came alive in his mind. A long time ago, when the first Dragon Seeker arose in the world, transformed by the magic that would set his destiny, a seed of knowledge was planted. And now it had bloomed.

Somehow, Duncan knew what to do.

"I don't know how, but I can do this," Duncan said. "But can I return you to this form?"

"Let's do this one step at a time," Gesselring said. "Once I succeed, if I succeed, we can deal with it then. Now we must hurry before the others no longer can stop the Red Dragon from destroying them all."

Gesselring smiled at his son, patting him on his shoulder, "be strong my boy, be strong." Then he took a few steps back.

"Ready?" Duncan said, still unsure of what was about to happen.

Gesselring nodded and closed his eyes.

Duncan rolled forward, raised his hands, and words came to him from deep within.

Chapter 64   Two Can Play the Deception Game

"What's happening?" Duncan said, his chair made it impossible to get close enough for him to see.

"Gesselring," Kathy said, "I mean the Gifrōren, is talking to the Red Dragon. The Manticore and Raven Queen are standing with them."

"Are they buying it?" Duncan said.

"Wait a minute will ya," Kathy said. "He just got there."

Duncan rolled his chair back, tapping his hand on the arm rest.

Kathy turned around to look at him. "The Raven Queen and Manticore are leaving with the raven army. The Red Dragon is still there. I don't think he's convinced him yet."

"Wait," Kristin whispered. "He is leaving, heading back toward where we hid the orb. Shhh! Quiet or he'll hear us."

As the Red Dragon faded into the distant sky, they all came out of hiding, dragging Duncan's chair over the rough terrain and back onto the trail.

The Gifrōren motioned for them to approach.

Kathy and Kristin went to Jamie, helping him to his feet as he came to. Duncan went to Destiny and the dragons.

"We don't have much time," Gifrōren said. "We need to get Destiny and the dragons out of here. Kathy can you and Kristin handle that?"

"Of course," Kathy said.

"Jamie, can you walk?"

The look in Jamie's eyes said it all. Between the fog of being out cold and facing a creature he once thought of as the enemy, confusion didn't come close to describing it.

"You, you're really on our side now?"

"No time to explain," the Gifrōren said. "Can you walk on your own?"

"Yeah, I can," Jamie said, backing away from the Gifrōren.

"Okay, go. I'll wait a few minutes in case they come back here early and discover the trick. I'll be right behind you after that."

*****

Templar met the band of rescuers outside the school. "I see the mission was accomplished. Now we need a new place to hide."

"Why bother, Mr. T? They always seem to find us anyway, "Duncan said. "Time we stop running and take a stand."

Templar nodded, "spoken like a true warrior, my boy. Okay, inside. Gather in the gym. There is only two ways in and no windows, we can easily keep watch."

Once they had the nest settled, and Destiny back among her children, Duncan told Templar what had happened.

"The Gifrōren should be here any minute," Duncan said, "he said he'd be right behind us. Then you can transform him back."

Templar remained silent.

Duncan studied his reaction. "Mr. T, what's wrong?"

"About that, Duncan, the ah, the transformation can only work once."

"Once? What do you mean once?" Duncan said, joined by Gesselroot and the others. "You turned him back before."

"There is a limit to the magic. A creature can be transformed into one form and then back, but only once. Any other transformation is permanent I'm afraid."

"What?" Kathy said. "But wouldn't Gesselring know that?"

"I'm sure he did," Templar said. "I'm certain of it."

"Then why…" Duncan said, his words interrupted by Destiny placing one of the baby dragons in his lap.

"For them, my boy, for them," Templar said, nodding to the dragon climbing on Duncan.

Duncan stroked the dragon's head, then rolled back to the nest. Gently placing the dragon back, he looked around. Something jumped out at him, then Destiny's voice came to him in his mind.

"You've seen what I've seen, Dragon Seeker, haven't you?"

"One of the dragons is missing," Duncan answered.

"Yes, the bold one who attacked the Red Dragon," Destiny replied.

"What do we do?" Duncan said.

"You and I shall seek out the Red Dragon and find my child."

"But the others won't let us go alone."

"Then we will have to find a way to leave without their knowledge. This is something we must do together, without risking the others."

"Let me go. You should stay with the other dragons."

"No," Destiny said, "we are responsible for them and together we shall find the missing one and return with him."

"What are you two up to?" Templar said.

Duncan looked at his teacher and mentor. Glancing at the nest without thinking, he knew by the reaction on Templar's face he'd given away their secret.

Templar bent down and whispered in Duncan's ear. "I'll take the others and check the surrounding area. Jamie and Keladry will stay here. When I leave, tell them what you're doing and leave them with the nest. They'll understand."

"You think so?" Duncan said.

"Well, Keladry will, and she'll keep Jamie under wraps in case he's stubborn."

"In case?" Duncan said.

"Okay, because he is," Templar answered, then stood, nodding at Destiny.

"Kathy and Kristin, with me. Jamie and Keladry talk to Duncan. Let's move."

Not giving anyone time to ask questions, Templar headed toward the exit with Kathy and Kristin in tow."

Jamie watched the others leave, then looked at Duncan. "Okay, what are you gonna tell me to do that I will not like and that I am not going to do?"

"Jamie, you can't argue about this. You and Keladry need to guard the nest and dragons. Destiny and I must do something alone." He held up his hand when Jamie started to argue.

"No discussion, Jamie. I need you to do this for me."

"Listen to him, Jamie," Keladry said. "There are things only a Dragon Seeker can do. I fear this is one of them."

"I don't know, Duncan," Jamie said. "Why can't I go with you?"

Duncan rolled over to face Jamie. "Because I asked you not to."

Jamie's shoulders slumped and he let out a long sigh. "Fine, but if you get yourself killed, I won't ever talk to you again. And I'm taking the flying OHRV."

Duncan smiled. "Thanks, pal. Take good care of the dragons."

Chapter 65   A Line in the Sand

"Where do you think he's taken the little one?" Destiny said, flying low over the ground, trying to stay hidden.

"Back to where this all began," Duncan said, clinging tightly to her neck. "He'll go to Diamond Hill. He knows we'll come to save the dragon. He wants us to come to him.

"I think there is mistrust creating a rift between him and the others. He must have taken the dragon as insurance against a double cross. Maybe we can use this to our advantage."

"Will he harm my child?" Destiny asked.

Duncan stayed silent, yet it spoke volumes.

In the distance, Diamond Hill rose from shadows of the late afternoon sun. Near the top of the hill, pacing back and forth, the Red Dragon was easy to spot.

"Do we try and surprise him?" Destiny said, circling lower, ready to land.

"No, he knows we're coming. Surprise isn't going to work. Fly right to him and let's finish this once and for all."

"Are you sure this is wise?" Destiny asked.

"I'm not certain of anything except we need to save that dragon."

Destiny gave a powerful flap of her wings, propelling them up the side of the mountain, landing in front of the Red Dragon.

"Ah yes, the mother and her protector come to save this runt of a dragon I see," the Red Dragon hissed. "How do you know it's not too late?"

Destiny tried to lunge at him, but Duncan held onto her wing. "No, Destiny, he's trying to separate us."

Destiny pulled back, glaring at the Red Dragon.

"Perhaps a little sport is in order," the Red Dragon grinned. "Let's see how far I can toss this pathetic excuse for a dragon, and you can try to get there before…well, before he sees just how dangerous flying into rocks can be."

Reaching behind a rock, the dragon yanked the struggling baby up in the air, dangling him by his tail. The baby snarled and tried hurling small streams of dragonfire, but it was too little to have any effect.

"Ah, the little one is feisty. Perhaps he needs to see what a real dragon can do with dragonfire."

Tossing the little one into the air, the Red Dragon reared back, prepared to unleash a torrent of flame.

Unable to hold Destiny back, Duncan watched in horror as the young dragon spun in the air trying to use its still unfamiliar wings.

Destiny flung herself at the Red Dragon, knocking him back. Duncan pushed himself hard and fast, catching the terrified baby just before it hit the ground. Taking the small one into his arms, and closing his eyes, he waited for the fireball to engulf them.

But something unexpected happened.

Nothing.

Opening his eyes, he realized he was alone with the baby dragon. Destiny and the Red Dragon were gone.

*****

"I should have known he would take her," Templar said. "The baby was just the bait to lure her back."

"But where would they go?" Duncan asked.

"That I cannot answer," Templar said. "Where else would he take her to gain an advantage over us?"

And once again the answer bubbled up in Duncan's mind.

"He's not taking her anywhere; he's coming here to us."

As the words left his lips, the sound of dragon's wings reached through the walls and chilled them all.

Chapter 66   A Choice without Options

"No!" Duncan said, rolling his chair in front of the door. "We should've known it would come to this. This is between me and the Red Dragon.

"If you guys try to interfere it will give him more to use against me. I can save Destiny, but I need to face this alone."

"No way!" Jamie said. "If you go out there, I go out there."

"I'm afraid he's right, Jamie," Templar said. "As reluctant as I am to say this, we cannot help Duncan. As the Dragon Seeker he must face the threats to his quest alone."

Jamie started to argue, then stopped. Kristin put her arm around his shoulders. Kathy came over to stand next to him.

Templar walked over to Duncan. "My boy, I'd hoped it would never come to this, yet it has. You are wiser than I suspected, recognizing and accepting your path. Be cautious, my boy. While you have skills and powers, they are no guarantee of success.

"Let's hope fate has chosen well."

Duncan glanced around the room. All these friends have stood by him throughout this ordeal. He knew each of them would go out there with him without question. But he also knew this was for him alone to do.

"I got this, Mr. T, I got this." He hoped his bravado was more than just words. Spinning his chair around, he rolled out the door, down the corridor to face the Red Dragon.

*****

"So, Dragon Seeker, you would believe sacrificing yourself for the greater good is a noble cause? Foolish little boy. Did you think creatures such as me would let some puny little chairbound wizard wannabe triumph over us? Such a foolish, foolish little boy."

The Red Dragon rose to his full height, pushing his foot down harder on Destiny's neck. "Shall I break her neck here, in front of you, and be done with it, or will you realize you cannot win?"

Duncan glanced around. There was little he could do from his chair; the Red Dragon was too powerful. But he had to think of something, maybe even just delaying him might help. Why is it he had to do these things alone?

A voice, soft yet familiar, reached his ear. He saw no one but knew what it had to be.

Two hippogriffs now hovered above the Red Dragon.

"All you had to do was think of us and I told you we would come."

"We? I thought there was only one of you?"

The larger of the hippogriffs drifted closer. "And here I thought you were already on to me." For a moment, the hippogriff faded and Ms. Wächterin appeared.

"Wait. You're a hippogriff too, Ms. Wächterin?"

"How do you think we managed to be in so many places? I am surprised you didn't figure it out." The hippogriff form reemerged. "Now onto our little problem."

Duncan was glad for the company but saw little they could do to help. "How can you do anything to stop him?" his word thoughts reaching out to the creature.

"We can do nothing, but you can. You have magic Duncan, you have powerful skills, but most of all you have the strength that comes with empathy and understanding. Think, Duncan, think. Why is such a powerful beast like the Red Dragon negotiating with you?"

And then it dawned on Duncan. The Red Dragon wouldn't hurt Destiny. He can't, he needs her to raise the little ones. And, he needs me too. Duncan rolled closer to the Red Dragon. His move caught the beast by surprise and, just for the briefest of moments, he saw fear in its eyes.

"Take your foot off of her now!"

The Red Dragon forced a laugh, "Or what?"

Duncan pulled his cellphone from his pack and pointed it at the dragon. "Or I will send you back in time to face an entire world of LAST Dragons."

The Red Dragon hesitated for a moment, then stepped back, releasing the struggling Destiny. She flew to Duncan's side.

"Now what?" she whispered in his ear, "isn't that the thing you talk to Jamie and Kathy on?"

"Yup, but he doesn't know that," Duncan said out of the side of his mouth, keeping the device pointed at the dragon.

For what seemed like forever, no one moved. Then, the Red Dragon, regaining his courage, started moving back toward Duncan and Destiny.

"You think you can intimidate me with that puny wand? What manner of wand is that anyway, a fool's wand?"

Moving closer, the Red Dragon reared back. Just as he appeared ready to pounce, Duncan hit the start button and loud music began playing.

The Red Dragon stopped dead in his tracks, backpedaled, then flew off into the clouds.

"Wow, who knew fear alone could overwhelm even the most powerful of dragons?" Duncan said, putting the phone back.

The Hippogriffs landed next to Duncan. "We told you it was always within you."

"It was a bluff. What if he didn't fall for it?" as he said the words, the music started again, Duncan hit pause.

"Music hath charms…" said the Hippogriff.

A noise drew their attention as the Raven Queen and her army of ravens encircled them. Destiny rose up to her full, if less than intimidating height. The Hippogriffs stood their ground.

Soon, the others joined them, forming a tight group around Duncan. Templar kept a sharp eye in the sky lest the Red Dragon return.

"So, Mr. Emeris, you've managed to frighten off the Red Dragon I see. No matter, I had little faith he alone would accomplish our goal." She took a few hopping steps toward them, then stopped when Destiny shot out a short but powerful flame.

"No need for the fireworks; I come in peace bearing gifts." The Raven Queen raised her wings in mock surrender. "I've come to grant you a special power, Mr. Emeris, in light of your recent success."

"I want nothing from you. Give me one reason I shouldn't have Destiny barbecue you right here."

"Well, I couldn't stop you," a tight-lipped grin crossed her face, "but I know that conscience of yours will. No matter, do as you wish, but I will still grant you this power." She tossed a small emerald onto Duncan's lap.

Duncan went to throw it back.

"No, Duncan, leave it alone." The hippogriff tried to stop him before he touched it, but it was too late.

Duncan felt warmth travel up his arm from the emerald as he closed his hand around it. Reeling back, he tried to throw it away, but it disappeared from his hand.

"There you go, Dragon Seeker, now you have another power at your command. With it, you can do anything, anything you like, including making your legs work again, but this magic only works once. One time you have the power to change the course of any event."

"I will never use any such dark magic from the likes of you, Harper."

"Never say never, Mr. Emeris." The Raven Queen let out laugh. "All you have to do is focus on what you want, and it will be done." Harper began to beat her wings as the flock of ravens took to the sky.

"The choice is yours, Dragon Seeker, wouldn't it be nice to walk again?" She leapt into the air and hovered for a moment. "Oh my, I forgot to mention one thing. Should you choose not to use this power within one year from today, it, and you, will vanish forever."

She gave a long, sinister laugh and was gone.

"I'm glad that's over," Duncan said, leading the way back to the nest. "None of that was true right Mr. T?"

"I'm sorry to say it is, my boy. She does indeed have the magic to do such things," Templar said.

"They'll be back?" Duncan said.

"If not them, then others I'm afraid. And now face another deadline, removing the magic the Raven Queen just put on you."

Duncan looked at the nest full of dragons, each of them full of potential to restore the dragons to the world. As he watched them play, oblivious to those who would do them harm, he was certain of one thing; he would protect them with his own life if needed.

"I'll be ready, Mr. T. I'll find a way."

"I have no doubt, Duncan," Templar said. "The role of Dragon Seeker could not be in more capable hands."

The End (for now)

About the Author

Joe Broadmeadow was born in Pawtucket and grew up in Cumberland, Rhode Island. He lives wherever his wanderings take him with his wife, Susan.

After twenty years with the East Providence, Rhode Island Police Department, he retired with the rank of Captain. He served in various divisions within the department, including the Commander of Investigative Services. He also worked in the Organized Crime Drug Enforcement Task Force and was on special assignment to the FBI Drug Task Force.

Imagination and writing have always played a big part in Joe's life. Starting with grammar school, Joe has been spinning stories for decades (just ask his wife.)

The LAST Dragon trilogy: *Saving the LAST Dragon, Raising the LAST Dragon, and Freeing the LAST Dragon,* are the culmination of decades of imagining a world where dragons and humans interact.

When Joe is not writing, he is hiking, taking pictures of the stars and planets, or fishing (and thinking about writing).

Joe completed a 2,185-mile thru-hike of the Appalachian Trail in September 2014. After completing the trail, Joe published a short story, *Spirit of the Trail,* available on Amazon.